THE PRINCESS AND THE FAWN

The Princess and the Fawn

DANIELLE HUGHES

FOUR MOONS PUBLISHING

Publisher: Four Moons Publishing
Author: Danielle Hughes

Cover design and chapter details: Dovnik Designs @dovnikdesigns

First Printing, 2023

For Derek

Our story takes place in a time long ago, and a land far away. Where the fairy tales we know today were once reality. When kings and queens reigned over their lands, and magic was not as uncommon as you might think. In fact, nearly every kingdom had their own sorcerer or sorceress, and witches and wizards were commonplace amongst the town's people. But with magic comes power, and with power comes corruption and greed. And like all good stories, this one contains a bit of each. But don't despair; there is also adventure and courage, and a dash of romance thrown in for good measure. But most of all, this is a story about the love of a brother and sister, and the lengths they will go to protect one another.

Prologue

Once upon a time... there lived a wonderful King and Queen who ruled over their land and lived harmoniously with the people who lived there. The Kingdom of Aldric was a safe and happy place and King Brennus and Queen Faelyn were admired and respected. After many years of trying to conceive a child, they were eventually blessed with a handsome little son they called Torin. A few years later they were once again blessed, but this time with a daughter whom they named Calia. Both children were beautiful, good natured and well mannered.

The family lived in bliss until Calia's fifth birthday when tragedy struck and the Queen became ill. No amount of medicine, healing or magic could save her and she eventually passed into the next world. Naturally, the children and the King were devastated and mourned her passing severely. After a year had past, the King became increasingly worried that his children were not moving on from their mother's death. They missed her so much. Especially Calia, who cried herself to sleep every night, clutching her mother's sunstone pendant which glowed orange in the sunlight. The King decided it was time he found someone to care for them in a way he couldn't. He decided they needed a mother. And so, the King remarried a seemingly kind hearted lady, who had lost her own husband a year ago, and had a daughter of her own.

The lady's name was Caradin and her daughter was called Avaleen. Caradin was a beautiful woman, tall and elegant, with chestnut coloured hair. Avaleen was not so fortunate. A carriage accident when she was small saw her face disfigured and the loss of her left eye. She always wore her ruby coloured hair draped across her face to cover the scar. Caradin walked with a staff to help with an injury she claimed she sustained in the accident that had left her daughter disfigured. The staff was long and elegant, like Caradin, with a shiny, black stone of obsidian on top.

The King and Caradin were married in an elaborate ceremony. While the townspeople embraced the new Queen, happy to see the King moving on, Torin and Calia were not to so quick to accept. In particular Torin, who was quite a good judge of character, did not trust his new mother. (He had overheard her speaking cruelly to the castle staff). And Calia had seen her kick some of the Castle's furry residents.

Soon after the wedding, the King's health began to decline. Some people said his heart was weak and never recovered from the loss of his first wife. After a slow illness the King too eventually passed, leaving behind his two precious children, in the care of their Stepmother.

After a small period of mourning the Queen's behaviour began to change. Her nature turned cold and unforgiving. She became short tempered, yelling at the castle staff often and belittling the children. While Avaleen could do no wrong, Torin and Calia seemed to do nothing right. They were constantly being reprimanded and punished for the smallest of misdemeanours. Eventually the children began spending more time with the staff of the household, who would have quit and moved on by now, but feared for the young Prince and Princess, and so they stayed to try and protect them in any way they could.

The Queen would not allow Avaleen to play with Torin and Calia, she was kept busy with lessons in music and art, and new toys to play with. If ever the Queen caught Avaleen playing a game like hide and go seek with her step siblings, Torin and Calia were punished, locked in their rooms for days at a time. And this is where our story truly begins...

Part 1

Whispers in the Woods...

Like most ten-year-old boys, Prince Torin hated being confined to his room. He was a curious and energetic boy who liked to be moving. Climbing trees, chasing the dogs, riding horses and playing stick ball were some of his favourite activities. None of which he could do when locked in his room. So, it was only natural that he would find a means of escaping when, for what seemed like the hundredth time, his stepmother had imprisoned him inside for another ridiculous misdemeanour. Torin flicked his pocket knife open and closed with one hand. It was the last thing his father had given him before he died. Torin's stomach grumbled and he pocketed the knife, the meagre provisions of bread and cheese his stepmother allowed him, were not nearly enough to support the appetite of a growing boy. And a prince no less. It wasn't right! He knew he was the rightful heir to the throne after the passing of his father, not Caradin. Although she already acted like she was the ruler of Aldric. Torin knew she didn't care for the people of the kingdom, she only cared for herself, and her daughter. And power.

Torin knelt on the seat below his large window and pushed the glass out wide. Carefully, he lowered himself down onto the stone ledge below, gripping the window pane with his fingers.

Don't look down.

It wasn't that he was afraid of heights, but peering down several stories to the garden below always made him dizzy and disoriented. Torin inched his way along the ledge until he reached Calia's window. Often, he would sneak into her room so they could keep each other company. Even though she passed the hours locked away easier than he did, playing make-believe and sketching, she did get lonely. But tonight, she was already curled up in bed, so Torin continued edging along until he came to the open window of the library. He was about to fling himself onto the armchair beside the window and sneak down to the kitchen, before he heard chanting on the breeze that rustled his hair. It was coming from further along the ledge, in the direction of Caradin's room. Momentarily forgetting his hunger, Torin continued edging along until he came to his stepmother's balcony. Leaning on the railing, he carefully peaked through a gap in the curtains and held his breath.

Caradin stood in the centre of her room, surrounded by black candles, all with flames flickering golden light. Her eyes were closed and she clasped her staff out in front of her, running a hand over the top of the obsidian stone. She wore a long dark cloak, but Torin could see her naked legs poking out from the join in the front. Caradin chanted words Torin didn't understand. As she increased the intensity of the incantation, the flames of the candles grew longer before turning a sickly shade of green. Caradin held the staff with two hands now, and Torin watched in amazement as an inky black shadow seeped out of the stone. The shadow took on the vague form of a tall, horned man. Caradin dropped to her knees, bowing before it.

'Master, I am gracious for your presence and seek only to serve you,' Caradin said to the wraith. Torin dared not move, straining to listen.

'What do you ask of me, in return for your loyalty?' The voice of the shadow came out like a deep, raspy drawl. A shiver of fear raced down Torin's spine. Every fibre of his being told him this was a demon.

Caradin glanced up at the demon, but remained on her knees. 'I ask of you, Dark Lord, for your guidance on taking the next steps to fulfil my destiny. To become the true Queen of Aldric. One who is most powerful and feared throughout the Kingdom.'

'You know what you must do. Kill the children, and you will be the rightful Queen. Feed me their souls and in exchange I shall grant you ultimate power.'

Torin's foot slipped as a piece of the ledge crumbled beneath him, his sweaty palm struggled to grip the railing.

'Great Lord of Darkness, the power I seek is superior to the power you previously granted. Will the souls of two children satisfy my request?'

The demon's size flared larger for a moment. 'The eye of a daughter granted you the power to see beyond what lies in front of you. The souls of two royal children will grant you the power you need to rule over the Kingdom, and ensure your subjects are loyal only to you. All shall fear you. All shall obey you. None shall ever leave you, should you desire it.'

The covetous smile which curled on Caradin's lips made Torin sick to the stomach. His life was in danger by a woman who mutilated her own daughter from her desire for power. Caradin was corrupt and it was clear she would stop at nothing to achieve her aspirations. Torin knew two things for certain. He and Calia where no longer safe in the castle, as long as Caradin was alive. And he was no match to stop her when she had magic and a demon on her side.

Torin watched as the demon reached a gnarled hand towards Caradin, and parted the front of her robe, revealing her naked body. 'Now it is time for me to fulfil my desire!' The demon growled.

Torin didn't wait to find out what happened next, he carefully crept back along the ledge to Calia's room. Using the pocket knife his father had given him, he unlatched her window and pushed it open, tumbling onto her window seat. Immediately, Calia sat up in bed, gasping in fright.

'Hush, sister. It is only me.'

'Torin, what are you doing?'

'I'm afraid I have something terrible to tell you.' Torin climbed into bed beside Calia, chilled from the night air and everything he just witnessed. He relayed his encounter, shivering, emphasizing his fear for their lives.

'We cannot stay here any longer, Calia. We must leave, tonight.'

'But where will we go?' Calia asked, her eyes wet with tears.

'I don't know. Maybe to the next Kingdom, Caedryn. Mother and Father often talked of the King and Queen there. I remember Mother saying she was close friends with Queen Niamh, they grew up together. They might be able to help us.'

Torin watched as the tears spilled down his sisters' cheeks. 'Pease don't cry, Calia. I promise I will keep you safe. As long as we stick together, we will be alright.'

'What about Avaleen?' Calia sobbed.

'Caradin didn't speak of harming of her again. I believe she will be safe. Caradin could have killed her at any time for power. But the fact she only sacrificed a small part of her, tells me she must love her daughter, in her own strange way.'

Torin watched as Calia clutched their mother's sunstone pendant. 'Come now sister, you must pack a small bag and put on your riding cloak. We need to leave tonight.'

'I want to say goodbye to Chevlon,' Calia said, opening her wardrobe, referring to the castle's cook. Chevlon had always cared for the children, ensuring they had enough food and hiding them when Caradin was on a rampage.

'If she's in the kitchen when we go down for supplies, you can. But the fewer people who know we're running away, the better.'

Torin packed his own satchel and put on his cloak, and the brother and sister snuck downstairs into the kitchen, keeping to the shadows. Chevlon was still awake, drinking whiskey with her feet up in front of the fire.

'I knew you two would be down for a snack at some stage,' Chevlon said, heaving herself out of her chair. 'But what's with the cloaks and bags, my darlings?'

Calia burst into tears and rushed to hug Chevlon around her ample middle while Torin, in hushed tones and whispers, quickly relayed to her what he had witnessed.

Chevlon shook her head with sad eyes. 'It will take you several days to walk to Caedryn, but I think it's the best thing to do for now. If anyone can keep you safe from that monster, it's King Fionn and Queen Niamh,' she said, bustling around the kitchen, wrapping up parcels of cheese and cured meat. 'But you should travel through the Woodland to prevent being detected. Once she realises that you're gone, she'll have guards out looking for you. The forest will keep you hidden.'

'I can get us there,' Torin said, his eyes wide. 'I will keep us safe.'

'You're a good boy, Torin. Your father would be proud.' Chevlon pulled Torin into a bear hug.

'Will you look after Avaleen?' Torin asked.

'Of course, I will. It's not the child's fault her mother is a monster.' A noise in the corridor caused them all to stop and turn. 'Just a mouse.' Chevlon assured.

Calia wiped her eyes. 'What about you?'

'Don't you worry about old Chevlon, my little love. You just get yourself to safety. Now get going, before someone else finds you out of bed. I'll see you again, don't you worry about that.' The three of them embraced one last time, before leaving the castle kitchen behind them, and disappearing into the shadows of the garden.

The castle's tall stone walls and drawbridge loomed before them. Torin led Calia along the wall to a side gate he was hoping was unmanned and they could sneak through. There were no guards around, but the gate was locked. Torin pulled out his pocket-knife to pick the bolt away when a crunch on the gravel stopped him. A figure emerged from the shadows.

'I know that you're leaving.' Avaleen called, stepping from the darkness into the light of a torch above the wall. Her long red hair shone in the light. She too had snuck out of bed that night, hoping for a midnight snack. Avaleen loved Chevlon, just as her stepsiblings did. Chevlon provided the warmth and soothing comfort of a kindly grandmother, the type of affection she never received from her mother. Avaleen had overheard everything.

The three children stood still, staring at each other.

'You won't tell on us, will you Ava?' Calia asked, eyes wide.

'She has to,' Torin said. 'Caradin will punish her if she ever found out Ava knew and didn't tell her. It's okay Ava, we understand.'

Avaleen's eye filled with tears. Torin and Calia were the only ones who called her Ava.

'You could come with us?' Calia suggested, hating to see Avaleen upset.

But Avaleen shook her head. She knew her mother was awful but the fear of angering her, scared her more.

'You'll have a better chance without me. No one will know who you are, but they will recognise me straight away.' Avaleen said.

Calia threw her arms around Avaleen's neck and squeezed her tightly.

Torin placed his hand on Avaleen shoulder. 'Wait as long as you can, okay? To give us a chance. Just pretend we're playing hide and seek. Now close your eye and count, as high as you know.' He said.

Avaleen did as Torin asked. When she reached higher than she had counted before, she opened her eye and stared out into the darkness. But there was no sign that her step siblings had ever been there.

~

Avaleen waited until dawn to tell Caradin. She wasn't surprised to find her mother already awake and getting ready for the day. When Caradin learned her step children had run away, she reached for her staff and began muttering strange words under her breath, caressing the stone until it swirled with a dark mist. The stone revealed the children running towards the large Woodland that bordered their kingdom. To Avaleen's surprise, her mother started laughing.

'Are you not angered by their escape, Mother?' Avaleen asked.

'Those children have made my plan even easier to carry out!' Caradin cried with wild eyes.

Avaleen watched as her mother opened a cupboard beside the fireplace and threw various ingredients into a large black cauldron hanging over it. Powders, herbs and potions were added until it popped with a large plume of green steam. Caradin leant over the cauldron and inhaled the steam deeply, then holding her breath she crossed to the window, leaning out into the dawn air. She exhaled, releasing the emerald mist, which expanded as it floated out across the land of Aldric. Avaleen kept her eye on the mist for as long as she could, until it seemed to settle over the dense treetops of the Woodland.

'Mother, what have you done?' Avaleen asked, a sick feeling in her stomach.

Caradin's mouth curled into a wicked grin. 'I've cast a dark enchantment over all the water sources for miles, so as soon as the children drink any water they will turn into defenceless animals.' Caradin strode to her dressing table and sat down. 'I'll now be rid of them forever, as they will not be able to speak and will be eaten by other wild animals, or hunted. No one will ever know.' Caradin began putting earrings on as Avaleen felt cold all over.

'I have plans to rule this land my way. I will announce to the Kingdom that the children have passed away from a deathly fever. And you, daughter, will help me convince everyone.'

Avaleen's hands shook as her mother strode to a locked cabinet beside the bed. She approached Avaleen carrying a small glass vile of purple liquid.

'You will drink this potion and it will give you symptoms of a bad fever. Don't fret however, it will last a day or two and you will be fine.' Caradin roughly cupped Avaleen's chin, pouring the bitter liquid into her mouth.

'Now, off to bed with you. I need to find someone to bring me the bodies of two children who can pass as those wretched runaways.' Caradin cackled as she ushered Avaleen out of her room, closing the door behind her.

~

The children ran as far as they could throughout the night without stopping. During the day they hid in the hollow of a large fallen tree until the cover of nightfall came and they ran through the Woodland again. Soon they had eaten all of their food and drunk all of their water. They had to stop at a river to refill their waterskins.

As they approached the rushing river Calia felt the chill of a cold wind on her neck, and heard whispers.

'*Beware!*' they repeated as the water lapped at the shore.

'Torin!' cried Calia, 'can you hear the trees whispering?'

Torin frowned. 'Don't be silly Calia, you're imagining it.'

'*Beware!*' leaves rustled on the wind, '*the water! Beware!*'

Calia grasped her mother's pendant. 'Really Torin, I'm not imagining it. The trees are telling us to beware of the water in the river. We shouldn't drink from it.' Calia clutched her brother's arm tightly.

Torin sighed. Calia had been through a lot and he didn't want to upset his clearly distraught sister any more. He agreed to press on.

The next day was hotter day by far, and the children needed water. Torin found a spring and stopped to fill their flasks. But again, Calia felt the chill and heard the trees whispering a warning.

'*Beware!*' they rustled, '*the Queen has bewitched the spring!*'

'Torin!' Calia cried, 'Please stop. The spring is dangerous!'

'Sister, I'm sorry but we must drink the water or we will die.'

Calia pled with her brother again, tugging him away, but he ignored her cries and drank from the spring. Just one sip at first, but the water was sweet and delicious. He guzzled it down in giant mouthfuls, unable to stop.

'See Calia, there is nothing to fear, the water is wonderful,' exclaimed Torin, but the look of horror on Calia's face, as she started to back away made him freeze.

The gentle outline of Torin's jaw and his creamy skin became blurred. Fur began sprouting all over his body. Torin cried out as his back elongated, his hands and feet twisting into hooves. His ears disappeared and new ones sprouted from the top of his head. His nose grew out and turned black.

'Calia! What's happening to me?' Torin cried, panicked. But Calia could not speak. For her brother had disappeared, and in his place stood a young grey fawn.

'*Calia, what is wrong?*' Torin asked again. But his voice was an incomprehensible bleat.

'Torin?' she asked.

'*Yes of course it is me. What is wrong with you?*' he demanded.

'You should have listened to the warning,' Calia cried, shaking her head. 'Look at your reflection.'

Torin peered over into the water of the spring and was shocked by what he saw.

'*Oh no!*' he cried, '*What will we do now?*'

Calia tentatively reached out and stroked the fur of her brother; she was surprised by how soft he felt. 'I'll look after you,' she whispered.

'*But who will look after you?*' Torin sobbed in response.

'We will stay together and look after each other.' Calia replied, 'Just like we planned'.

Calia and Torin found cover and curled up together and slept until night fall.

The brother and sister travelled one more night, with Torin carrying Calia part of the way because she was so weak from lack of water. Eventually, she had no choice but to drink or she would die. Torin easily found a small waterfall, hearing its gentle trickle from afar. He led Calia closer, nudging her. The trees were quiet and so Calia drank the water. Nothing happened. Calia lapped at the water before cupping her hands and drinking more. Glancing around the forest, Calia noticed unfamiliar flowers and plants. They must have crossed the border into the next kingdom and be far enough away from their evil step mother's magic. The caw of a raven overhead urged the children on, for fear they could still be spied upon.

In the deepest part of the Woodland, the pair came across a rundown old hut, and decided they should seek shelter there. After everything that had happened, in fear, both children believed it was too dangerous to seek the help of the neighbouring kingdom. Caradin was clearly extremely dangerous and powerful and they didn't want anyone else getting hurt, or get themselves caught.

Now that Torin was a fawn his hearing and sense of smell were more sensitive and he could tell if any creatures or people were coming close to them before Calia could. But no one ever came, and so they lived there peacefully for several years. Calia tidied the hut, repaired it and tended the garden; she'd had lots of practice from living under her stepmother's rule. Torin searched the woods bringing back roots and berries for Calia, and sometimes he was even able to catch a rabbit for her to eat. Calia learned how to fish, and hunt for small game. The siblings were able to communicate, as if by magic. Calia could hear Torin's voice in her mind and he could still understand her. The two made a great team. Overtime Calia grew into a beautiful young woman, and Torin grew into a magnificent stag, as large as a horse with antlers that towered above his head like a great tree. And for the most part, they were happy, and safe.

Part 2

The Silver Stag

Once upon a time... in the Kingdom of Caedryn, there lived a wonderful royal family. King Fionn and Queen Niamh ruled fair and just and were admired among the people. Their two children, Prince Evander and Princess Luna were loved and respected. But the King was growing old and tired and wished to abdicate to his son, and the Queen was dreaming of grandchildren to fill the castle with laughter and mischief. It was time for Prince Evander to take over, to marry and settle down, but as often happens when one tries to force such things, the perfect bride had so far eluded the handsome Prince.

'I don't understand why I can't rule alone, Father? I'll undergo the coronation and begin my duties as King, and when the right woman presents herself, then I shall marry her.' Evander said over dinner one night. The young prince brushed his dark hair back off his forehead, then reached for his wine.

'It's tradition, Evander. I was married before I became King, as my father was and his father before him and so on for as long as our reign goes back.' King Fionn explained.

'What if you were to die, right now? What would happen then?' Evander queried, his blue eyes sparkling.

'Evander!' gasped Queen Niamh. 'Do not speak of such things, you'll put a curse upon us, wishing things like that.'

The Queen had hair the colour of honey piled on top of her head, with small streaks of grey at her temples.

'I would never wish such a thing, Mother. I was merely proposing a possible scenario to prove my point. If Father were to die now, I would take his place as King, unwed, and childless.' Evander explained.

The King sat back, resting his hands on his large belly. 'Being King is harder than it looks, son. The pressures are constant. One needs a life aside from running a Kingdom to keep his mind from obsessing over decisions and dilemmas. A wife and a family provide joy in a life that can easily become taxing and stressful.' King Fionn reached for his wife's hand.

'I can't imagine Ev married to anyone; it would be quite funny really. Who could put up with him? Honestly, he's so annoying.' Princess Luna said, smiling. She had the same dark hair and blue eyes as her brother.

'Speak for yourself, sister. It will be your turn soon enough.' Evander said, flicking a pea in her direction.

'I'm not getting married. Astrid and I have already decided we're going to live together on a farm, in a lovely cottage, with lots of animals.' Luna said, flicking the pea back towards her brother.

King Fionn sat up straighter. 'Now there's a good match. Astrid is a great girl, and at least you could take her hunting with you. The girl has stealth and accuracy better than any huntsman I've ever met!' King Fionn suggested, rubbing his salt-and-pepper beard.

'Astrid can't marry Ev, she's my best friend!' Luna cried looking shocked.

'Don't worry Luna, if I marry Astrid, you can come and live with us and have your cottage and your farm.' Evander said with a wink.

The sibling's eyes met over the floral centrepiece on the dining table. Evander knew Astrid would never consider marrying him when her heart belonged to someone already. And he could never break his sister's heart like that. It pained him to think what would happen in a couple of years when her parents started trying to find potential suitors for Luna.

'Perhaps I could at least speak to her father, see what his plans are for his only daughter?' King Fionn said.

'It couldn't hurt.' Queen Niamh said. 'Evander?'

'Can I at least celebrate my twenty-first birthday before we have to decide? Then I promise I will start taking the whole marriage thing seriously.' Evander said. Although Evander knew it was his duty to become King, and he wanted to fulfil that duty very much, deep down his heart yearned for an adventure. He knew he lived a privileged life, that he was grateful for, but he couldn't ignore the longing for a thrilling and reckless escapade before he had to become serious and settled.

The King and Queen eyed each other.

'Very well.' The King agreed. 'Now, what sort of celebrations are we talking about here? A grand ball? Perhaps we could kill two ravens with one stone and your perfect wife will sweep you off your feet on the night?' The King chuckled. 'It's happened before you know.' King Fionn smiled at his Queen who blushed.

'I really don't need a ball, Father. I was hoping to host a hunting trip instead.' Evander said, sipping his wine.

'A hunting trip?' The King repeated, scratching his beard. 'What sort of hunting trip. You can go hunting any day you like, son.'

'Not a regular hunt. One where we camp out until we find something really special. A proper send off to farewell my boyhood and welcome the encroaching responsibilities of manhood.' Evander said.

Luna snorted and choked on her own wine.

'What's so funny?' Evander cried.

'Encroaching manhood? Why don't you just be honest Ev, you want to hunt the Silver Stag and behold the glory of the one to finally catch the mythical beast.' Luna said.

'Is this true, son?' asked the King.

'I'm not saying that's specifically what I hoped for, but if I happened to come across such a creature, it would certainly make for a fantastic birthday present.' Evander said.

'Finding the Silver Stag is as elusive as finding the perfect wife, but if that is what you wish for your birthday, then so it shall be. Let us know the guest list, and we'll arrange invitations. Now, can someone please pass me that pudding.' The King said.

~

The day of Evander's birthday hunt arrived. There were ten people in the hunting party including Evander, his best friend Dunkley, Astrid and several other close friends. Luna had come to see them off, hugging Astrid tightly, their embrace lingering for several moments. Evander watched as Astrid tucked a stray lock of hair behind Luna's ear.

'You make sure you look after Astrid,' Luna said to her brother, giving him a peck on the cheek.

'You know as well I do that Astrid can take care of herself. She's by far the best hunter here.' Evander replied, glancing over at Astrid, readying her horse. Astrid was tall and athletic, with skin the colour of cocoa and silky, dark hair like his sisters.

'Yes, but I worry with her being out in the Woods with only your friends. It's not right for a lady to be spending several nights camping with only male companions.' Luna exclaimed.

'Luna, to us Astrid is a friend. No one sees her as anything other than one of the boys. We all know she could knock us out with a single punch. Remember that party when that foolish drunk Count kept trying to drag you into another room? Astrid clocked him on the chin before I could take more than two paces. He was out cold for the rest of the night!'

'I know, just please be careful, Ev.' Luna said.

'Of course, sister. We'll see you in a few days' time, hopefully with a grand prize to show for it!'

Luna made a disgusted face, she hated hunting. But she understood the lure of the Silver Stag. Men had talked about hunting the creature since she was a little girl, when stories started sprouting about the fabled creature being spotted in the Woodland which bordered their Kingdom. It was around the same time that the neighbouring Kingdom of Aldric closed its borders after King Brennus died. The rumours were that his new Queen was so heartbroken by the death of her husband, closely followed by the death of her two young stepchildren from a horrible fever, that she couldn't bear the rumours that began to sprout immediately.

When the townspeople began suggesting foul play was at hand, the Queen feared for her life and that of her daughter. She enlisted the help of a sorcerer to close the borders to their Kingdom forbidding anyone in or out. The Kingdom of Aldric was now surrounded by an enchanted mist, so powerful that if you were to enter it you would become horribly disfigured and lost forever in a foggy limbo, never to be seen again. The common belief was that the Silver Stag had come from the mist, and that if you were to capture him, you would hold the power to clear the fog and free the lost kingdom.

~

Evander's hunting party travelled through several villages on the first day, spending the night at an Inn, before heading off again the following day. There was a popular marketplace in the town located on the border of the Woodland, where the legendary Silver Stag was said to reside. Evander was hoping to spend the night nearby and pick up some information from the locals on the best places to go to spot their prize.

It was early afternoon when they reached the marketplace, which was still bustling with people trading, buying and selling goods, catching up on the latest gossip. Evander and his party drew quite a bit of attention when the locals realised the prince was in their midst. Evander spent an hour greeting people and convincing them to treat him as a regular visitor. It didn't stop the vendors all vying for his attention, hoping he would spend lots of money at their stalls. Evander had to promise that either he, or a member from his party, would purchase something from each merchant as long as the people promised to leave him be. Eventually, the attention died down enough that Evander was able to roam the Marketplace freely.

Dunkley and Astrid stayed by the prince's side while their other friends wandered off. Partly because they were his closest friends, and partly to protect his Royal Highness, a direct order from the King. They stopped at each stall they passed to browse, and as promised, pick something out to purchase. The prince asked each vendor to store the purchased goods until he passed through on his return from his hunting trip.

At a stall selling handmade jewellery, Evander helped Astrid pick out a delicate floral broach embedded with opals for Luna. The stones reminded him of the moon for which his sister was named, and their mother's favourite gem, moonstone. The Queen always wore her favourite moonstone pendant under her clothing.

While Astrid was paying for the brooch, a high, tinkling laughter caught Evander's attention and he turned towards the next stall, where the sound had come from. The laughter belonged to a young maiden with deep-golden hair, and when she turned around in Evander's direction, he was rendered frozen, for she was the loveliest woman Evander had ever seen. Her long amber coloured hair hung in loose waves cascading down her back, small sections pulled back at the sides to stop it from falling in her face. Her large, dark blue eyes were framed by thick lashes, her lips full and soft. She smiled when their eyes met, gently bowing her head in his direction. It was several moments before Evander could concentrate again, and the maiden had returned to wrapping up a parcel for a customer.

Dunkley's tall form stepped in front of Evander, waving an olive-skinned hand in his face.

'What's wrong with you?' he asked, stepping past his friend.

'Um, nothing. I was just, um, nothing,' the prince said.

Dunkley and Astrid both smiled at Evander when they realised what, or who rather, had so intently captivated his attention.

'Go and talk to her.' Astrid nudged him on the shoulder.

'What? Oh no, you go.' Evander said.

Astrid laughed. 'I just bought something, it's your turn now.'

Dunkley and Astrid wandered ahead to the next stall giving Evander some space. The young maiden glanced at Evander again, making his cheeks burn as he realised he was still staring.

'It's alright, there's no need to purchase anything from me. I'm sure the last thing a Prince needs is a posy of dried wildflowers.' The maiden called in his direction.

It took Evander another moment to find his voice. He watched as the maiden played with a stunning golden stone around her neck before tucking it inside the neckline of her dress. Astrid and Dunkley were motioning for him to move.

'Nonsense.' Evander eventually said, taking a step in the direction of her table. 'I happen to love wildflowers.'

'Is that so?' The maiden asked with a smile. 'And which would be your favourite then?'

'Oh, the um, you know. The purple ones there.' He said, pointing to the closest bunch.

'Violets?' The girl asked.

'Yes, violets, of course.' Evander said, feeling his cheeks flush. He had never been caught so off guard by a woman before. He straightened his jacket and tried to regain his composure. He noticed there were other items for sale at the maiden's stall, herbs, fruits and vegetables and some hand carved wooden animals. A carving of a stag caught his eye.

'Did you make this?' Evander asked, picking up the wooden animal.

'I did.' The maiden replied, stepping to stand opposite Evander.

'I hear there is a legend of a magnificent Silver Stag which resides in the Woodland.'

The maiden smiled. 'It's just a silly tale, a bedtime story to tell children.'

'But what if it weren't just a story?' Evander asked. 'Imagine what a prize it would make the lucky hunter to capture such a beast. He'd be celebrated throughout the entire Kingdom.'

The lovely smile left the maidens face. She took a step back from the table.

'Is that why you're here?' she asked.

'My friends and I are planning a hunting trip in the Wood-land, yes.' Evander said. The maiden's brow furrowed. Per-haps she was offended like Luna, at the prospect of hunting animals for sport.

'To hunt the stag?' she asked, her blue eyes boring into his.

'Stags do make for excellent hunting. I'm not going to pretend otherwise. And if the legendary Silver Stag were to show himself it would make for even better sport.' Evander replied.

'Would you like to make a purchase? I have other custom-ers to attend to.'

'I'm sorry if I have offended you, it certainly was not my intention. Please will you accept my apology?'

'Of course, your highness.' The maiden replied with a formal bow.

'Perhaps a gesture, in good faith, to prove how sorry I am to have upset you? I would like to purchase the entire contents of your stall, please.'

'That really is not necessary.' The maiden replied.

'I insist, and it would be my honour.' Evander said, placing a pouch of coins onto the table. 'This should be more than enough to cover the costs.'

The maiden glanced at the pouch of coins and then back to the prince.

'I'm sorry, your highness, but my items are no longer for sale.' The maiden replied curtly, throwing a large linen cloth over the entire table to cover everything except the pouch of coins. 'I am officially closed for the day.'

The prince stood staring; his mouth open in confusion. How had this ended up going so horribly wrong? He turned around to find one of his friends arguing with another vendor, seemingly over the price of a leather belt. When he turned back to the maiden, she was gone.

~

Calia raced towards the Woodland, pulling her hood and cloak tightly around her. She glanced back once to ensure no one was following, before slipping through a small opening in the trees that led to the path home.

'Torin?' She called to the forest around her. He often waited nearby on market days to walk home together and carry her baskets on his back or wedged between his antlers. Though today she had left in such haste.

'Torin?' Calia called again. She had been quite enjoying the company of the prince until he'd mentioned the Silver Stag. He was no ordinary stag; his colouring was unique. Calia had never seen, or heard of a deer with a coat so light grey in colour it resembled the mist which settled over the Woodland on a wintery morning, or antlers that were pearlescent and gleamed when the sunlight hit them. He was also much larger than a full-grown stag. Even if it wasn't for his colouring, his sheer size would still make him a prize among those who hunted for fun.

'Torin!' Calia called again, louder this time. The prince certainly lived up to his reputation of being tall, dark and handsome. Hair as black as coal, eyes as blue as a bright summer sky, with skin like ivory. She felt foolish to even entertain the thought that the prince had seemed interested in her more than her wares, but she had noticed him staring at her. Even though she knew nothing would ever come of it, it had been nice to have held his attention for a short time. But none of that mattered. She needed to warn Torin about the hunting party.

Calia was well into the midst of the Woodland and still no sign of Torin. She wondered if she should turn back in case he was waiting for her near the marketplace. But she was worried if she did, she would lose her lead on the hunting party.

'Argh, Torin! Where are you?'

Calia heard his voice in her mind before she saw any sign of him.

'*What are you doing all the way back here?*'

'Oh Torin! Thank goodness,' Calia cried, glancing all around her for a sign of her brother amongst the trees, but he was very good at blending into his surroundings, even though his coat was so light in colour.

'*What's going on?*' Torin asked before stepping onto the path in front of her, munching on some long vines as they dangled from his mouth.

'Torin, we need to get home immediately. The prince is at the market with a hunting party, they've come especially to hunt you down.' Calia cried, hurrying towards him.

'*Plenty of hunting parties have come looking for me and never been successful. Why are you so worried?*'

'Because it's the Prince, Torin! And all of his high-born friends. People who have been trained in hunting for sport since they were children. People who have the best weapons and resources for tracking and killing whatever they desire.'

'*Sounds like it should be great fun, I love a good run around.*'

Calia walked past, reaching up to grab his ear, pulling him in the direction of home. 'This isn't a game Torin, it's serious. People like the prince are used to getting what they want, they won't leave until they find you.'

'*You mean people like us?*' Torin said, refusing to budge. Calia turned and gazed into her brothers' eyes, the same dark blue as when he was human.

'We haven't been those people for a very, very long time. I barely even remember what it was like to live in a castle.'

'*Then perhaps it's time you were reacquainted?*'

'What are you talking about?'

'*Would it be so bad if the prince found us? This could be your chance to tell our story, to live the life you were born to live. Don't you want better than living alone in the middle of the woods?*'

'I happen to like our home in the woods, and I'm not alone, I have you. And the marketplace. Besides, no one would ever believe our story, Torin. We have nothing of proof.' Calia considered her brother for a moment. Not a day went by that she didn't feel bad for him having to live his life as a stag, especially on the days she attended the market, or when he was being hunted.

Calia reached for the smooth fur on her brother's neck. 'If we walk into the Kingdom of Caedryn, and claim to be who we say we are; me a grown woman, and you a giant stag, they will have us locked up or thrown out.' Calia said, trying to make Torin see reason. 'The last time you didn't heed my advice brother, you ended up like this.' Calia motioned to her brothers cervine form.

Torin stamped his hoof and snorted, flaring his nostrils at the reminder. He had always been proud, and disliked being reminded of his mistakes.

'Go home sister. I do not need you to tell me what I should do, nor do I need you to look after me.' Torin turned, leaping into the dense forest, and disappeared amongst the trees. Calia released a frustrated sigh, and continued on the path back to their home in the woods.

The cabin had changed a lot since they first discovered it, all thanks to the hard work of Calia, under the instruction of Torin. It now had a wrap-around porch and a barn like structure attached to the left-hand side, as Torin's antlers could no longer make it through the doorway. A pebbled path of river stones which led from the front door, was bordered by garden beds of wild flowers. The back door also had a path which was surrounded by beds of herbs and vegetables. A short fence of thatched branches surrounded what the siblings considered to be their property, before being swallowed up by the density of the surrounding forest. In the ten years they had lived there, their home had never been discovered by another person. Torin was sure to always lead any hunters away from their hut, and they were so deep in the woods, no one ever ventured close enough to discover their home.

As Calia made her way down the pebbled path to her front door, thoughts of the prince and his crystal blue eyes, churned in her mind with the annoyance that he and his hunting party had caused this tension with her brother. She wondered when Torin would return, promising herself she would apologise immediately. It wasn't unlike him to disappear for a day or two before returning home. Calia hoped he wouldn't stay away too long just to spite her warning and keep her worrying. Which he did have a tendency to do after an argument. Or when he needed time alone to sulk in his own dark thoughts, before returning, happy and nonchalant as though nothing had ever happened.

~

Calia awoke the next morning to the dissonant sound of a horn some distance away. Her heart sped up and her stomach dropped: those horns only meant one thing. The prince's hunting party had spotted their prize. Instinctively, Calia rushed outside her back door, to stand on her porch, shielding her eyes from the morning sun as she peered into the depths of the woods. She could see nothing, hear nothing. Whatever was happening was too far away. Folding her arms across her chest, Calia grasped her mother's sunstone pendant, running her thumb over its smooth surface. She knew the sound of the horn meant the hunt was on. But it was the sound of the trumpet she dreaded the most. For when the brassy notes of the trumpet resounded through the air, it meant the hunt was over, and that the hunters had caught their prize.

Throughout the day, the sound of the horn carried on the wind several times. And each time Calia's heart pounded in her chest, as she wiped sweaty palms on her apron. She tried to keep busy, tending to the gardens, mending the roof, gathering what she could. But time dragged as though every passing minute was an hour. The sun sank lower, and only when it disappeared was Calia able to relax. And although she barely slept all night, at least she knew Torin was safe as the party could not hunt in the dark.

Calia rose with the sun, cursing her stubborn and proud brother and the pompous, selfish, arrogant prince. For it was his fault she had fought with her brother in the first place. Even the first deep call of the horn didn't abate her anger.

'I hope he gets caught,' Calia thought to herself. 'It would serve him right.' But immediately she felt terrible and took back her words. Of course, she didn't want that. What she wanted was for this whole ordeal to be over.

At midday, Calia retreated inside to make herself some calming tea atop the cast iron, pot-bellied fireplace which kept her small home warm in winter. Before the water could boil, shouts carried by the wind drew a prickle of fear up her spine. No such sound had ever been heard from within her home before. More shouts followed, along with the thundering of hooves and crashing of shrubs and branches being demolished by horses and their riders. As she ran to the window, Calia watched with a mixed sense of dread and relief as Torin came pounding out of the Woodland, leaping over their fence in a single bound. He stopped mere inches away from the front door, his antlers scraping against the eaves of the roof. Calia stayed hidden and watched as men on horseback pulled up just short of the fence line, their faces a mixture of triumph and tired relief at having finally cornered their prize, and confusion at the discovery of a cottage so deep in the woods. Torin's breathing was heavy but he was not frightened at all.

Calia heard his voice in her mind. *'Now it is time that I took care of you, sister.'* He slowly stepped off the porch and out into the openness of the garden, bowing his head low, while Calia clutched at her chest, withdrawing from the window. What did he think he was doing? He was giving himself up!

From within the copse of trees, a large grey stallion broke out, the prince upon his back, a victorious smile on his handsome face. He wiped sweat from his brow as he pulled an arrow from a quiver at his hip, notching it into his bow.

'At last, you are mine.' He called, just loud enough for Calia to hear. She watched in alarm as the prince drew back on the notched arrow. Calia was just about to open her door, when the prince suddenly lowered his bow.

His friend approached. 'Why do you not strike?' he asked.

'It hardly seems right, Dunkley, to slay the beast while he stands here, in this garden. It's like he's given up. The win does not seem as grand with him standing in wait, not putting up a fight at all.'

Calia released the breath she was holding.

'But is this not what you wanted? The most sought-after prize in the past ten years? The beast many believed to be a myth, now stands before you, ready for the taking. Perhaps he has given up because he deems you worthy of his capture?' Dunkley suggested. Evander took a moment to consider the words of his friend, before raising his bow and arrow again.

Torin pawed at the ground, glancing at the cabin. '*Now, sister!*'

This time Calia didn't hesitate. Throwing open her door and leaping to stand between her brother and his would-be captor.

'Stop!' She cried. 'You cannot slay this beast!'

The prince and his men stared in shocked awe. Evander frowned, lowering his bow, recognising her at once.

'And why, may I ask, is that?' Evander asked.

'Because he isn't a beast at all. He is my brother.'

Part 3

When the Sun Meets the Moon

Evander stared at Calia, as resounding laughter from his friends filled the garden. Had it been anyone else to burst from this secluded cabin in the woods, and make such an outlandish claim, he too would have joined their laughter. But he could see the truth in the maiden's eyes, her determination to protect the Silver Stag. Evander held up his hand to silence his companions, before returning his arrow to its quiver and dismounting from his horse.

Evander held his arms wide. 'No one is to harm the stag,' he called to his friends. 'By order of the prince.' He watched the maiden relax, lowering her arms from shielding the beast. The stag let out a snort and turned, walking towards a trough of water beside the cottage.

'We meet again,' Evander said, offering the maiden a polite bow. 'That's quite a claim you've made on the beast, ah stag,' he said, correcting himself, not wanting to offend her a second time. Her dark blue eyes darted from him to his friends surrounding the garden. 'May I ask your name?'

Tell him the truth. Torin's voice entered Calia's mind and she shook her head in response to him. A quizzical look came over the prince's face.

'Very well, then allow me to introduce myself. I am Prince Evander, son of King Fionn and Queen Niamh, rulers of the Kingdom of Caedryn.'

The maiden continued to stare at him with wide eyes. She seemed uncertain, but not afraid.

'May I ask what makes you believe the stag to be your brother?'

Again, her eyes darted from him, to the beast, to his companions.

One of the prince's party called out ,'This woman is nothing but a witch, hiding in the woods. She has no claim to the beast. Hurry up and have your way with her Evander, then kill the beast so we can go!'

As Evander turned to scold his friend, the Silver Stag reared up and leapt to stand in front of the maiden, aggressively pawing the ground and snorting in challenge. In one swift move, Astrid and Dunkley dismounted, swords drawn before their feet hit the ground.

'Whoa!' Evander called, taking two steps back from the stag. 'Call off your beast.'

'Torin, stop.' Calia spoke, placing a hand on her brother's back.

'I mean you no harm,' Evander said, 'I do not share the sentiments of my idiotic friend. However, I must ask, did your stag understand what he said?'

Calia released a heavy breath. 'Yes,' she said through closed eyes, clearly reluctant to be answering his questions. 'My brother's name is Torin, and I am Calia.'

Evander frowned at Calia, understanding those names were obviously meant to mean something to him. Astrid's eyes widened in recognition.

'Of the Kingdom of Aldric?' Astrid asked, slapping Evander on the shoulder.

'Is it true?' Evander asked.

Calia's hair had fallen across her face, hiding her eyes from his gaze. She nodded softly, relieved her blushes were concealed. 'Yes, it is true.'

Calia brewed multiple pots of tea for Evander and his party while she told the prince, Astrid and Dunkley her story of how Torin came to be a stag, and they came to live in the Woodland. Evander told her what he knew of Queen Caradin, and the Kingdom of Aldric. How Caradin ordered for the Kingdom to be surrounded by an enchanted fog which no one could go through without becoming horribly disfigured, or lost forever. Only one heavily guarded road led in and out of the Kingdom for trading purposes. No one ever left and no one ever entered. Anyone found trying to sneak in or out was ordered to be killed. Formal requests had to be made in writing in order to address Queen Caradin and most were usually denied. After so many years, people in the surrounding kingdom's had given up trying to contact family inside Aldric.

'That is terrible,' Calia gasped. She had heard rumours in the marketplace, but mostly avoided becoming involved in conversations for fear of her identity being discovered. 'But unfortunately, I'm not surprised. Caradin is a terrible woman, and she is a powerful sorceress. I have no doubt she has created that fog with her own dark magic. Those poor people, trapped. It's not fair,' Calia said, her eyes brimming with tears.

They're our people, sister. We need to do something.

Evander watched as Calia turned to the window, where the magnificent stag stood, keeping watch.

'Can you communicate with each other?' Evander observed.

'I can hear Torin's voice in my mind, and he can understand everything we say.'

'What is he saying now?'

'He says that we should do something to help the people of Aldric, that they're our people.'

Astrid stood, stretching her long limbs. 'Technically, he is the rightful heir to the throne.' She nodded towards Torin.

Dunkley spat out a mouthful of tea, holding back a laugh. 'I'm not sure too many people would be happy with a giant deer on the throne, even given the current predicament!'

'You're such an ass, Dunk. Obviously, the curse needs to be broken first, you twit.' Astrid frowned.

'Do you think that's even possible?' Calia asked.

'Only a sorcerer or sorceress would know. We have one who works for my father,' Evander said. 'But it would mean you would have to come back with us.'

Calia shook her head. 'It's too dangerous. If Caradin finds out we're alive, she will have us killed. It would put your entire kingdom at risk.'

It is worth the risk. Tell them we'll go with them.

'We can offer you protection,' Evander said.

'No,' Calia cried.

'You don't want protection?' Evander asked, a puzzled expression on his face.

'I'm sorry, it's a generous offer, but it's too unsafe for all of us,' Calia tried to explain, struggling with the two conversations.

I'm going to go anyway, whether you come or not.

'You're a stubborn fool, is what you are!'

Everyone looked to Calia in shock, believing at first she was addressing the prince, until they noticed her attention was aimed outside.

'This takes some getting used to,' Evander scratched his head. 'May we be privy to your conversation?'

'I'm sorry, your highness, we're not used to company. My brother wants to come with you, despite my *warning*,' Calia glared in the direction of Torin.

'We shall give you a moment to discuss, while I rally up my friends. We've imposed on you too much already. But please, consider my offer.' Evander took Calia's hand gently in his own. 'It is not right that you should both have to live this way, when Caradin is the one at fault. I vow to offer you the protection and aid of the Kingdom of Caedryn, should you choose to accept it.' Evander bowed slightly before motioning to Astrid and Dunkley to leave.

Calia strode over to the window. 'Why did you have to bring them here? You've ruined everything!'

I'm doing what is right, for you. You should be finding a husband, starting a family of your own. You should be living the life of a princess. Not living in a hut, hiding in the woods. It may be too late for me, but not for you.

'I don't care for those things; I just want us to be safe.'

*We can be safe **and** you can still have those things, if you go with the prince. And if there's a chance the curse can be broken, I'm going to do everything in my power to take down Caradin and free the people of Aldric. Our people, sister!*

Calia closed her eyes, and turned away from her brother, before glancing around her humble home. It was true, she had often daydreamed about having a family of her own, but the fear of losing her brother or facing Caradin again always disintegrated those thoughts.

If you won't do it for yourself, at least do it for me, please. And for Aldric. Our father would never have let something so terrible happen to his people.

A knock jolted Calia out of her thoughts. She opened the door to Prince Evander, her insides swirling with un-certainty. Was she ready to give up the safety and solitude of their home? Was it time to reveal their identities and the truth to the world?

'Have you made up your mind yet?' Evander asked.

'Yes,' Calia sighed. 'We will come.'

~

The journey back to the castle took two days and such a spectacle had never been caused in the Kingdom of Caedryn before. There was no alternative but for Torin to walk out in plain sight, with Calia upon his back, amongst Prince Evander and his companions. People lined the streets for a glimpse at not only their prince, but the fabled Silver Stag.

The group spent the night at an Inn named Grimms Lodge, where Calia refused to leave Torin in the stables alone and insisted on sleeping beside him. The Inn's owner and staff bent over backwards to make them comfortable, knowing that having the Silver Stag and the Prince both stay at their Inn would only bode well for future business.

Evander, torn between the comfort of a clean bed inside the Inn, and keeping Calia safe, gave into his desire to prove himself worthy of Calia's trust, and slept in the stall beside her and Torin while Astrid and Dunkley kept guard overnight. Neither of who were happy with the arrangement, but their loyalty and duty to their friend came first.

Travelling through the last village before the castle, Calia watched everything in fascination, as though through the eyes of her much younger self. As they rode the pathway before Evander's castle came into view, frantic butterflies riddled Calia's stomach.

'I'm regretting this already, Torin,'

You worry too much, Sister. This is the right decision. Please trust me.

'You cannot know that for sure. King Fionn could turn us away, despising the danger we place him and his Kingdom in. He may send us straight back to Aldric. He may order us killed!'

I've observed the prince, from a distance. I've seen how he interacts with his friends; heard how they speak of him. He is a good man and I trust he will keep his word to help us.

Calia began to chew on her lip, pulling out her mother's pendant from under her cloak and running her thumb over its smooth, sunset coloured surface.

Evander rode up beside Calia. 'That's a lovely piece of jewellery,' he nodded in the direction of her pendant. Calia was quick to tuck it away out of habit.

'It's the only thing I have left from my mother. She gave it to me before she died. I've never taken it off.'

'My mother has one of similar size, but hers is white, not peach,' Evander said, looking towards the castle, now looming ahead of them. 'Home sweet home.'

Calia took in the expansive view in front of her, an enormous, grey-stone castle complete with turrets and towers and a drawbridge. Her stomach clenched.

'You have my word, fair Calia, you will come to no harm here,' Evander offered her a warm smile, but it did little to abate the sense of dread which had settled over her.

Trumpets sounded the return of the prince and his hunting party as they crossed the lowered drawbridge. Calia took note of the guards who stood at attention, their eyes following her and Torin as they passed, but their heads never moved. The hooves of Torin and the horses clopped loudly on the cobbled stone leading to the entrance, where a crowd of silent people stood staring. Calia's stomach dropped as she took note of King Fionn and Queen Niamh, at the front of the gathered crowd. Both wore expressions of astonishment.

Evander dismounted and crossed the distance, to be met with his mothers' open arms and a kiss on both cheeks.

King Fionn grasped his son by the elbows. 'I'm glad to see you well, my son. I see your hunt was a success,' He glanced over at the stag. 'But why is the beast still alive?'

'And why is it being ridden by a young woman?' Added Queen Niamh.

'Well, that is rather a long story, and I am in much need of a meal and an ale before I begin telling it,' Evander replied.

'Very well. Take the beast to the stables!' Kink Fionn commanded.

'No, he will be coming inside with us,' Evander said, glancing back to the nervous looking Calia and Torin.

Queen Niamh gasped.

'Yes mother, inside the castle. Please ensure our new guests are made comfortable and I promise I will explain everything.'

As the king and queen turned back towards the castle, looks of bewilderment on their faces, Evander motioned for Calia and Torin to approach and follow him inside. The gathered crowd muttered in whispers as Evander shooed them away, leading Calia and Torin inside and towards the dining room. From a staircase came a squeal as Princess Luna rushed down to meet them.

'I can't believe you actually did it! What is going on, brother? Where is Astrid?'

'Astrid is outside taking the horses to the stables. If you hurry and fetch her, you can join us in the dining room so I can explain,' Evander said.

Luna eyed Calia inquisitively, but offered her a kind smile before rushing off to find Astrid.

Once gathered in the dining hall, King Fionn took his seat at the head of an expansive, wooden table. Queen Niamh, Luna and Astrid sat, while Evander took a seat opposite them, a few spaces away from Calia. Torin filled up the space at the end of the table. A crystal chandelier hung above, sending flickers of sparkling light around the room while the scraping of heavy chairs echoed around them as everyone settled.

Evander launched into his tale of how he and his friends spent two days chasing the elusive Silver Stag through the Woodlands, only to end up in the garden of a young maiden who claimed the Stag was her brother.

'And so, I would like to take this opportunity to introduce to you Princess Calia and Prince Torin of Aldric.'

A collective gasp resounded from the table, followed by silence, before King Fionn stood up from his chair, the wooden legs scraping loudly on the tiled floor.

'You can't be serious, son. You expect me to believe this girl and beast are the children of the late King Brennus?'

'Yes, Father.'

'Why, just because this pretty girl told you so? You must be out of your mind, boy. What are you then, girl? A witch? Have you cast some spell over my son to convince him to bring you here? Well, let me tell you, girlie. You won't fool me in such a way! Call for the guards!'

'Father, no!' Evander cried, at the look of terror on Calia's face. 'Please, you must hear their story. Mother, please?' Evander beseeched.

The queen placed a calming hand over her husband's. 'Perhaps we can let her talk. It can't do any harm to hear her story.'

King Fionn looked at his wife with a frown. The queen whispered, 'she does bear a striking resemblance to Queen

Faelyn. Please let her speak. If we detect any lies, we can call the guards immediately.'

King Fionn roughly slumped in his chair. Queen Niamh commanded, 'Go ahead, child. Tell us your story.'

Calia had never told another soul their story. She took a shaky breath before beginning with their mother's death when Calia was just five years old, and her father marrying Caradin, and how their life turned upside down when their father died. Calia told Torin's tale of witnessing Caradin communicate with a shadowed demon, who promised her power in exchange for the souls of the children, and how they chose to run away when they learned of Caradin's plans to kill them. Calia finished with their escape, and retold how Torin ignored her warning not to drink from the spring. She explained how they have been hiding in the Woodland ever since.

Calia had been looking at her hands for most of the story, but raised her head upon finishing to see The King, Queen, Princess, Prince and Astrid all staring at her. A flush burned from her cheeks to her neck.

'A wild and terrible tale indeed,' King Fionn said, frowning in Calia's direction. 'But unfortunately, at this stage, it is just that. A story. I'm afraid we have no real proof of who you claim to be. No way of knowing for certain.'

Calia closed her eyes, lowering her head, her worst fear coming true. She turned to Torin, standing very still behind her. 'I told you this would happen.'

But it was not Torin who responded.

'Show him your pendant,' Evander said, leaning onto the table. Calia turned to face him, confused.

'What do you mean?'

'Show my father your pendant, the one you hold when worried.'

Calia hesitated while the King interjected. 'What could a pendant possibly prove?'

Suddenly Queen Niamh sat up straighter. 'Please dear, show us your pendant.'

Calia reached to her throat, tugging the silver chain around her neck, drawing her mother's sunstone pendant from the neckline of her dress. 'My mother gave me this before she died. She said as long as I was wearing it, she would always be close by. But I'm not sure what help it can be.'

Calia reluctantly pulled the chain over her head, never having taken it off before. She passed the pendant over to the queen, who immediately turned the apricot-coloured stone over. Gasping, she held it to her chest.

'I believe you, Princess Calia.' The Queen embraced a surprised Calia. 'I'm so sorry child, for everything you've had to endure. I vow to keep you safe from now on.' The Queen then reached up to stroke Torin's neck. 'And I believe you are Prince Torin.'

'Am I the only one confused here?' The King croaked.

'Forgive me, my love,' the Queen rushed back to the table, handing the pendant to her husband, before pulling her own chain from around her neck. 'You see, when I was girl, Faelyn and I were the best of friends. When we weren't together, we would write letters to each other, and we would always spend the summer together. We even became married in the same year and gave each other these pendants as parting gifts, as we knew our new lives as Queens would mean we couldn't see each other as often.' The Queen held the two pendants side by side. Hers showed a large, round moonstone, nestled in a silver crescent moon, while Calia's was a sunstone, the centre of a carved silver sun. Queen Niamh turned both pendants over to reveal the same engraving, a crescent moon circling a sun. 'We always said we would pass these onto our own daughters, who we hoped would grow up together and become the best of friends, just like we were.'

Calia raised her eyes to meet Luna's, and they shared a smile. King Fionn however, still appeared sceptical. 'What is it that you want from us?' he asked.

'Please, your Highness. We only ask that you grant us permission to consult your royal sorcerer, to see if the curse on my brother can be undone. We expect nothing more from you,' Calia said.

'Very well. I shall grant you that request.'

Torin scraped a hoof roughly on the tiled floor.

'But that is not all,' Evander interrupted, understanding. 'Something needs to be done to bring down Queen Caradin and free the people of Aldric. We must send soldiers there to defeat her.'

'I'm sorry, son. But a woman of such dark power will be no match for soldiers and swords.' King Fionn said gravely.

'What if we enlist the help of the Sorcerer? Perhaps he can tell us what sort of magic we are dealing with and offer a solution to break through it?' Evander asked. But he could tell by the grim expression on his father's face and his shaking head that King Fionn did not agree. 'It is the right thing to do, father. Would you not hope for help from neighbouring kingdoms if it were the people of Caedryn being held captive by a tyrant ruler, unable to escape for fear of death?'

King Fionn considered his son's words for a moment, both proud of his son's sense of justice and worried about the possibility of going to war against a dangerous and dark sorceress. 'Let us first consult with the Sorcerer to determine exactly what evil we are dealing with, before making any decisions.'

~

While a messenger was sent to fetch the Sorcerer, Calia was shown to a guest room and Torin was taken to the biggest stable the castle had to offer. Calia hated being parted from Torin, but Queen Niamh insisted he would be safe and cared for and kept under guard. Torin encouraged her to go, and enjoy the luxuries the castle had to offer.

When Calia entered the vast chamber of her guest room, she couldn't help but stare open-mouthed. Rich wall paper in ivory and gold covered the walls, with a window-seat providing a view of the gardens below. An enormous four-poster timber bed took up most of the space, covered by a richly woven duvet in burgundy and gold. She ran her hand over one of the many silk cushions adorning the bed, admiring its delicate fabric. But the best part was the ceramic bathtub situated in the far corner of the room, brimming with steaming hot water. Calia hadn't taken a proper bath in a tub since running away and wasted no time stripping off her riding cloak and tattered dress and settling into the soothing hot water. Calia barely even registered when a maid of the castle entered, scooping up her old clothes and laying new garments on the privacy screen.

By the time Calia emerged, soaped, scrubbed and probably the cleanest she'd been in ten years, the bath water was tepid and milky with soap suds. The new dress was cream and dusky rose in colour, and made from the softest and tightly woven linen and satin Calia had ever touched. Settling herself at the dressing table to brush out her half-dry hair, Calia barely recognised herself. At first, she thought it was her mother staring back at her from the mirror and she grasped her pendant for comfort. A knock at the door interrupted her thoughts.

'May I come in?' Princess Luna asked, opening the door slightly.

'Of course,' Calia replied, standing and offering a small curtsy.

'Oh please, you don't need to worry about such formalities, you are after all, a princess yourself,' Luna said, with a kind smile. Her dark hair and blue eyes matched her brother's. She looked every bit the princess in a pale blue lace gown, her hair falling in soft waves down her back.

'I don't feel like a princess,' Calia said, feeling nervous, smoothing out her dress.

'Well, that doesn't mean that you aren't one. And at least now you look the part,' Luna said with a wink. 'Shall I do your hair for dinner?'

Calia's initial reaction was to say no, but Luna was already ushering her back to the dressing table and opening drawers, pulling out an array of jewelled silver pins and combs.

'Sit,' she motioned to the settee.

Calia obliged, trying to sit up straight.

'I warrant it's been a long time since you've been dressed up and had a meal in a dining hall, after hiding in the Woodland for so many years,' Luna remarked.

'I barely even remember my life before,' Calia replied quietly.

'Do you remember your parents at least?' Luna asked, separating sections of Calia's hair and braiding them.

'I remember their faces, their voices. I remember the way my mother smelt, like rose petals and vanilla.'

Luna smiled, encouraging Calia to continue. 'I remember my stepmother being cold and cruel. Nothing I did ever made her smile. In the end, I remember feeling ill whenever she would come into a room.'

'How awful,' Luna said, twisting the top section of Calia's hair at the back of her head.

'And I remember Avaleen, Caradin's daughter.'

'The one with only one eye? How dreadful for a mother to do such a thing to their own child!'

'Avaleen wasn't like her mother. She was scared, like Torin and I, but she was never treated badly or punished. If she was caught playing with us, we would be reprimanded, not her.'

'It sounds like she may need rescuing from that awful woman too. There, what do you think?' Luna stood back, admiring her work, holding up a small mirror, while Calia twisted slightly in her seat to see the back of her hair. The top section was braided and twisted into an elaborate bun, fastened with a glittering comb, while the rest cascaded loosely down her back.

'It's lovely, thank you.'

'Shall we head down to dinner together? The Sorcerer arrived not long ago so they should be nearly ready for us.'

Calia stood while Luna linked arms with her and led her out the door.

The dining hall looked different in the evening, lit up with candles and a roaring fireplace down one end. Evander, Dunkley and Astrid were already seated at the table and stood to welcome the girls when they entered. Calia couldn't help but blush noticing Evander's mouth drop slightly open as he stared at her. She lowered her head, feeling self-conscious. Luna giggled.

'Close your mouth, brother, should you catch a fly in it,' Luna led Calia to the seat opposite him.

'Forgive me,' Evander smiled. 'Calia, you look lovely. I trust you found your room comfortable?'

'It's wonderful, thank you.' Calia took her seat, avoiding Evander's gaze. Luna cleared her throat, fishing for her own compliment.

'You look lovely too, sister,' Evander responded with an eye roll.

'As always,' Astrid chimed in with a wink in Luna's direction. Luna blew her a quick kiss before taking her own seat.

The echo of hooves across the tiled floor turned everyone's attention to the entranceway, as Torin entered, following behind two guards, who bowed stiffly before taking a stand outside the doorway.

'Are you alright?' Calia asked.

I am fine. You look wonderful sister; I see castle life is already suiting you. Torin nodded in the direction of the table before settling himself in front of the fireplace, tucking his legs underneath himself.

The King and Queen arrived next with the Sorcerer, a tall and thin man holding a long wooden staff and wearing a black cloak and matching black pants and boots. His dark hair was tied at the nape of his neck. He looked quite stark against the regal pair in their matching attire made of royal blue and gold satin.

'May I introduce Sorcerer Iván,' said the King, before taking his seat at the head of the table. Iván nodded curtly before veering to Torin by the fire place.

Torin made to rise before Iván held up a hand to stop him. 'It's true, you understand my words?'

Torin nodded his antlered head once to show his perception.

'May I?' Iván held out a hand, reaching for Torin's head. Torin nodded again, keeping his head lowered as Iván placed his hand on the stag's forehead and began muttering under his breath. Everyone watched, silent, waiting anxiously for Iván's diagnosis, while he held his staff over Torin. Several moments passed before Iván stood, shaking his head and frowning. 'I have seen the moments which led to this man's condition, and I can attest that this is in fact Prince Torin and Princess Calia. But I'm afraid the news is not good.'

Calia's stomach dropped at Iván's words as he strode to the table, taking his seat beside the king.

'This type of curse is rooted in the darkest of magics. From what you have told me, this Sorceress has bound herself to a demonic source, channelling its power. The curse will only be broken when she removes it herself, or is dead.'

A collective gasp went up from the table as Calia clutched at her pendant. 'Is there no other way?'

'A sorcerer's magic is tied to them. For every spell they cast, a personal sacrifice must be made in return for the power taken,' Iván started. 'Average witches and wizards are born with an innate attunement to the elements. They can perform small spells and enchantments, infuse elixirs and balms with healing abilities, that sort of thing. But a sorcerer takes their craft to the next level. They practice being able to find and draw out more power, usually from the natural world.'

Iván held the audience captivated as they listened to his explanation. He gulped a mouthful of red wine from a chalice before continuing. 'Myself, for example, I have learned to draw power from the earth beneath me, the molten lava and rock buried deep underground. I can also draw energy from the ocean, and winds of a storm. But in return, my own energy is depleted, and large spells require me to rest for great lengths of time to recover. For some, the desire for power becomes too great, and the natural world does not suffice their craving for more. So, they turn to sources dark and foul to supplement their greed. Demonic forces care not for the energy of living witches or wizards, but for the souls of a sacrifice instead.'

Shocked sounds and horrified expressions claimed the occupants of the dining hall.

'Outrageous!' King Fionn exclaimed. 'Not only has this woman been allowed to practice dark magic, cursing people, maiming her own child. But she is sacrificing lives in the process?'

Iván nodded solemnly.

'What can be done to stop her?' Queen Niamh asked.

'Aside from killing her, her link to the demon would need to be destroyed,' Iván said, reaching for a dinner roll.

'What does that involve?' Evander asked.

'A sorcerer must use something to channel their power, both inwards and outwards. That is why most of us carry a staff, it is the perfect conducive device to direct energy.'

Calia sat up straighter. 'Caradin has a staff, she was never without it. Only hers is black wood with a claw at the top encasing a dark stone.'

'Obsidian,' exclaimed Iván. 'The blackest of stones for the darkest of magic. Besides killing her, that stone would need to be destroyed to sever the link to the demon, and her power. Until that is destroyed, she will be more powerful than an army of sorcerers, let alone soldiers.'

'Are you saying it would be no use to send a legion of soldiers to take back the land of Aldric?' King Fionn asked.

Iván shook his head. 'A sorceress as powerful as this Caradin will be no match. She will obliterate them with a wave of her staff. You'll need a much more cunning plan to bring her down.'

Castle staff entered the dining hall carrying trays and plates of food which they set down in front of everyone. The aromas wafting from the dishes set Calia's senses alive; the scents of roast meat, gravy, potatoes and vegetables, the likes of which she could barely remember eating, but her stomach told her she was in for a treat. Her meagre meals of the past ten years of flat bread, berries, carrots, beans and small game could not compare. It was all she could do to stop herself shovelling everything into her mouth at once.

'The initial challenge is getting into Aldric in the first place and past that deathly fog,' King Fionn said between mouthfuls.

'Are you saying you're on board then, father? That you agree with freeing the people of Aldric?' Evander asked.

'I can no longer sit idly by, knowing innocent people are being sacrificed for her hunger for power. What's to say she won't come for us next?'

Use me as bait.

Calia glared sharply at Torin, ignoring his words. She watched in horror as he stood up from his resting place beside the fire, shaking his antlers for attention.

Tell them. Use me to gain entrance to Aldric.

Calia frowned defiantly and shook her head at Torin, but Evander and Astrid where watching her intently.

'Calia? Does Torin have something to say?' Astrid asked.

Calia closed her eyes and sat back in her chair. Torin stamped his hoof loudly on the tiles.

'He wants to use himself as a way to get access into Aldric. Use himself as a prize, or offering.'

Dunkley chimed in. 'No one knows his true identity. But the legend of the Silver Stag is known throughout all the neighbouring Kingdoms.'

Calia shook her head. 'It's too dangerous. She may kill him on the spot just to mount his head on her wall!'

'There may be another way,' Evander started, looking at his father.

'The proposal?' King Fionn asked.

Evander nodded. 'About two years ago, we received a letter from Caradin, proposing a betrothal between her daughter and myself, as a way to join the kingdoms and bring about an alliance.'

'No doubt a ploy to gain access to our land so she could work on taking us over! I'm certainly grateful now you refused to even consider the notion, or meet the girl!' King Fionn said, pouring rich gravy across his entire plate of food.

'Perhaps we could send a letter first, explaining a review of the proposal? Now that I'm older and coming to the age where I'm more seriously considering taking a wife. We could suggest I attend the castle to meet with Avaleen, as a means to get us past the fog?'

'Evander, that seems a very big risk, going into enemy territory. This woman sounds deranged and dangerous!' Queen Niamh pressed her hand to her heart as though the mere thought caused her pain.

Evander placed a hand on her arm. 'Mother, this situation is going to require both bravery and sacrifice. I'm willing to do it, if it means we can stop her. Torin and Calia deserve to be reunited with their homeland and people, and sitting on the throne, not living in fear.'

Luna scoffed. 'This plan is going to need a lot more thought than just getting you into the castle. What will you do then? You can't just walk up and snatch her staff from her!' she said.

King Fionn clinked a spoon against his glass. 'Let's just send the letter first and see what comes of it. She might refuse, and we'll be back to square one. Now a toast, to our guests. And to courage, and to truth. And to fighting for what is right!' As King Fionn raised his glass and took a sip of wine, everyone around the table followed suit.

Calia glanced between Torin and Evander, who were both watching her, and she wondered why men had to be so damn foolish, with their bravery and courage. Even though she knew Caradin had to be stopped, she just wished with all her heart, that it didn't have to be at the expense of good people who had done absolutely nothing wrong in the first place.

~

A letter was sent to Aldric the following morning, explaining that since their last correspondence, the prince had matured somewhat and reconsidered the previous offer. King Fionn mentioned that while his son had many suitors to choose from, so far none seemed the right fit. The letter outlined the attributes of Prince Evander, and what the kingdom of Caedryn had to offer Aldric, should such an alliance come to fruition. A request for the prince to enter Aldric, to meet with Caradin and her daughter was made. The messenger was instructed to deliver the letter to the guards at the only entrance into Aldric as swiftly as possible, and wait for a reply before returning. It was possible for the journey to be made in a day, but they knew they wouldn't have a response for at least three days allowing for the return journey.

Torin roamed the castle grounds, and enjoyed the gardens and orchard. He wanted for nothing, being provided with the highest quality feed and treated to daily grooming. Calia was free to enjoy the indulgences of the castle, being treated like the princess she truly was. On the first day, Luna organised a dressmaker to take her measurements, and Calia was presented with endless fabric options to have new dresses made for her. She had no idea about the current fashions, nor what colours suited her, so let Luna choose, much to Luna's delight. Calia hoped to spend the afternoon exploring the castles expansive library, having had very limited access to books. But was instead waylaid by Luna who had plans for a doubles game of croquet with her, Astrid, and Evander.

'We often play a game on a nice afternoon, but Dunkley has gone home to visit his mother so we need another player,' Luna explained.

'I haven't played since I was seven, I doubt I'll be any good,' Calia felt a nervous knot in her stomach at the thought of making a fool of herself.

Luna linked her arm through Calia's. 'Not to worry, Dunkley is hopeless anyway, so you haven't very big shoes to fill. Besides, Evander is a great teacher, he can show you some tips.'

Calia had an inkling Luna had orchestrated the game with an ulterior motive.

'So, I'm to be on Evander's team?'

'Well, you can't very well be on my team, Astrid can get terribly jealous, you know.'

Calia wasn't buying it at all, but allowed herself to be pulled through the castle and led out to the garden, secretly excited by the prospect. She was pleased to find Torin sunning himself out by the rose bushes, looking relaxed and content.

'Hello, brother.'

Good afternoon, sister. I hear a game of croquet is about to take place. That should provide for some pleasant entertainment. You were never very coordinated, you know.

'I'm already nervous enough, I don't need you making it worse.'

Torin's voice chuckled in her mind.

'You're starting to look a little round in the belly there, dear brother. Enjoying the spoils of royalty, are you?'

If anyone deserves to indulge a little, it's me. Oh look, here comes your Prince Charming, ready to dazzle you with his ball hitting skills, no doubt.

A flutter of nerves spread through Calia as she nervously tucked her hair behind her ear.

You look fine, stop stressing. It's a game after all. It won't kill you to have a little fun.

'Princess Calia,' Evander smiled and bowed in Calia's direction. 'Now, I have no idea what Luna has said to you, but

Dunkley and I are the reigning champs against these two, and I intend to keep it that way. Are you up for the challenge?'

'I hate to disappoint you, but I haven't played since I was a small child, so I may not be the competitive partner you desire.'

Evander held out his arm for Calia and she placed her hand lightly in the crook of his elbow. 'I believe you will make the perfect partner.'

Calia felt lightheaded as Evander led her towards Luna and Astrid, waiting in the shade of an umbrella, sipping iced tea. Evander handed her a wooden mallet with a long handle and indicated where to stand, lining the ball up in front of her.

'Shall I show you how to hold the mallet?' Evander asked.

'I need all the help I can get,' Calia replied.

'First of all, stand side on, feet apart for good balance, and let your arms hang long.'

Calia felt awkward holding the handle of the mallet, unsure where to position her hands. Evander stood behind her, reaching his arms around, and placing his hands over hers. Calia's breath caught in her chest.

'Place your hands like this,' he gently manoeuvred her fingers until one hand was slightly lower down the handle, the other resting above. The touch of his soft, slender fingers on hers made her shiver.

'Now, the key is to swing the mallet, not your arms as much. It's more in the wrists.'

Evander held his hands over Calia's and swung the mallet back slightly, before flicking their wrists forward and tapping the ball. The mallet made a satisfying 'clunk' as it collided with the ball, sending it rolling towards the first hoop. It came to a stop a few centimetres away.

'Not bad for your first try!' Evander exclaimed, resting his hand in the small of Calia's back for a few seconds. The warmth of his palm could be felt through her dress and Calia missed it when he moved away. Evander poured a glass of tea, offering it to Calia as Astrid took her turn. Calia waited in the shade of the umbrella.

Evander whispered to her, 'Now, you see how Astrid is leaning forward. Don't do that. She's completely off balance and is going to overshoot the ball – Ha! See I told you!' Calia giggled as Astrid's ball sailed past the hoop instead of going through.

'You're in the best position to hit your ball through first,' Evander said when Calia picked up her mallet for her next turn. 'Just hit the ball nice and easy.'

Calia made sure to hold the handle as Evander had shown her, and tapped the ball a lot more lightly this time. It sailed easily through the hoop, and Evander let out a loud 'whoop!'

'The first point goes to us!' he cried, wrapping an arm around her shoulders and squeezing her gently. 'See, perfect.' His smile was infectious and Calia couldn't help but return it. Their eyes locked for a few seconds until Astrid broke the spell.

'Well, the next one will be going to us. You can count on that!'

The afternoon progressed in the most delightful way, and Calia felt she was living in another world. She couldn't remember feeling happier or more relaxed, sipping iced tea, joking and laughing with the others. She didn't even notice until after the game was over that Torin had left his place under the roses. She looked around the garden for him, but he was nowhere to be seen.

While the others returned to the castle to rest before dinner, Calia took herself off to the stables to find Torin. She had a feeling that watching her enjoying the afternoon may have caused him to become depressed about missing out. It wasn't uncommon for Torin to go through a spell of despair every now and then, when he became frustrated and fed up with being trapped as a deer. Her instincts served her correctly, and she found Torin curled up in his stable.

'I didn't see you leave the game, are you alright?' Calia asked, stepping around antlers to find Torin's face. His eyes were closed, but she could tell by his breathing that he wasn't asleep.

I left when it became obvious you were going to win. Evander seemed pleased with himself.

'It seems they take it quite seriously,' Calia started before Torin began burying his large head in the hay.

'I'm sorry you couldn't join in. I suppose it couldn't be much fun watching, an unwelcome reminder of our current predicament.'

My current predicament, you mean.

'Don't be like that, Torin. We are in this together, like always.'

Except that you are free to go about and live your life, while I am at best going to roam the gardens and get fat.

Calia gave a sigh. She knew these types of discussions never ended well and that whatever she said would only go around in circles. Torin would have a deflection for any positive words she offered.

'I wish as much as you that you weren't like this. And hopefully with the help of King Fionn and Evander, you won't have to be. For the first time in a long time, we have hope, Torin. And that should count for something.'

No matter what happens with the proposal, I want to go back home and face Caradin. I've seen what life can be like for you, you don't even need to return. But I will be going back with or without the support of Caedryn.

Calia wanted to shout 'no'. But she knew it wouldn't make a difference. And Torin had every right to do as he chose.

'Just promise you won't do anything without discussing it with me first. I want to support you however I can. And if you decide to go back and face Caradin, then I want to help you do that. We have always looked out for each other, Torin. Always. And I'm not about to stop that now.'

~

The reply from Caradin arrived the following evening during dinner. King Fionn read the scroll to himself, his lips moving silently. Torin rose to attention from his place beside the fire, as everyone seated at the table waited like statues. Queen Niamh, Evander, Luna, Astrid, Dunkley and Calia all stared at the King, who frowned before placing down the scroll.

'The good news is that she has agreed to meet with Evander for an initial assessment of his suitability for her daughter,' King Fionn paused, turning to look at Torin. 'The bad news is, word has spread of the capture of the legendary Silver Stag, and she requests for him to be presented as a gift to the Kingdom of Aldric.'

Everyone began talking at once, except Calia who turned to her brother.

This is a good thing. This is what I want.

'No, Torin. She must already know that it's you.'

Not necessarily. She is greedy and covets that which is most prized. She only wants me so she can lay claim to the legend.

'I will be going with you,' Calia said.

No, you should stay here where it's safe, where you are guaranteed the life you deserve. Let Evander and his company take care of this.

'I will not stay behind and hide again. I want to see Aldric restored as much as anyone else - ' A hand on her arm caused Calia to stop abruptly. She suddenly realised the room had gone quiet and all eyes were on her. The hand belonged to Evander.

'I'm guessing Torin has agreed to come as said offering, and that he is trying to convince you to stay behind?'

Calia could only stare between Evander and Torin, while Torin stamped his front hoof and nodded his large head up and down.

Evander took Calia's hand. 'Calia, you are free to make your own choice. If you want to stay behind where it's safe, you will always have a home here, no matter what,' Evander turned to his mother who nodded in agreement. 'But if you want to come with us, I will not turn you away. In fact, I think your help could be of great advantage.'

'Does this mean you have a plan, son?' King Fionn asked.

'Yes, but I need to know who is willing to come first.'

Dunkley raised a hand. 'I will be by your side.'

'As will I,' Astrid confirmed, with an apologetic glance at Luna, whose disappointment showed on her face.

'I too, will come,' Calia said.

'I will also arrange a small regiment to accompany you,' King Fionn said. 'Caradin has advised only a total of ten people will be allowed to enter the kingdom. And there's something else you should know, before we hear your plan.'

'What's that?' Evander asked.

'Caradin has stated that the Stag must be caged upon entry into the kingdom.'

'No!' Calia gasped. 'Torin is a man, not a wild animal. We cannot cage him!'

'I think the decision should rest with Torin,' Evander said, giving Calia's hand a squeeze.

Calia pulled away and turned to her brother. 'Torin, surely you don't agree with this!'

If being caged gets us inside Aldric, then I agree.

'But you'll be trapped. The whole thing could be a trick and you'll have no chance to even try and escape. She could kill you on the spot! Please, Torin. I beg you!'

Right now, all that matters is getting inside the kingdom. Unless we can do that, we have absolutely no chance of ever defeating Caradin. I have to do this.

Calia placed her head in her hands, the hopelessness of the situation weighing on her like a bag filled with sand.

'I promise we will do everything we can to protect Torin.' Evander said.

Luna rushed from her seat to wrap her arms around Calia. 'I know it feels hopeless, but I believe my brother will do everything he can to keep your brother safe. And my father's soldiers are strong, and loyal. They will protect Torin.'

King Fionn cleared his throat. 'Perhaps we could hear your plan now?'

'Very well,' Evander started, tearing his eyes away from Calia's hunched form. He felt terrible seeing her upset. 'I'm hoping there won't be a need to protect anyone. In that, my plan is to keep Caradin believing we are on her side, and wanting to meet her demands for the proposal to be a success.' Evander turned to Calia. 'No one knows the castle better than Calia, so if she agrees, I thought we could disguise her as one of the soldiers. Once we are inside, when the time is right, Calia can slip away and hide. While we keep Caradin and her daughter entertained, proving myself to be the perfect suitor, Calia can hide and wait for an opportunity to steal Caradin's staff and destroy it by smashing the stone. With her power gone, the cursed fog will lift, and the full force of our troops will be able to enter Aldric and defeat her army, if she even has one left once her power is gone.'

King Fionn nodded, 'It seems like a good plan. I will speak with Sorcerer Iván and see if he can aid you with protection from her magic. And I will have the troops on standby, should we not hear from you within three days of you entering the kingdom. I say we proceed.'

'Calia, what do you think?' Evander asked tentatively.

All eyes turned to Calia, wiping tears from her cheeks. 'I agree.'

~

For the next few days, King Fionn and Evander went over every possible scenario they could think of to keep their small troop safe. Iván provided them with two very rare, enchanted sweets. When bitten, the sweet would turn the consumer invisible for roughly an hour, enough time to escape and hide from a dangerous situation. As only ten people were permitted to enter Aldric, the plan was for Iván to provide a glamour potion for Calia to use, to make herself look like Dunkley. Dunkley would use one sweet to become invisible. When it wore off, Calia was to use the other to disappear and hide within the castle.

The castle blacksmiths and carpenters worked swiftly to build a cage on wheels large enough to house Torin and his antlers. The first time Calia saw Torin testing out the prison, her eye's filled with tears. She had an impending sense of dread since King Fionn had received Caradin's reply. She knew this was the only way to gain entry into Aldric and to have any sort of chance at taking back their kingdom, but Calia couldn't help feeling they were walking into one giant trap. It seemed like there were too many obstacles. But Calia was determined not to be left behind. And above all, she wanted redemption for her brother and their people. Torin deserved to have his curse lifted, just as much as the people trapped in Aldric deserved to be free from the reign of Caradin.

～

The morning the group of eleven, plus Torin, set out, the sun was shining in a blue sky. It seemed almost laughable that in two days' time they would be walking into what could be the end for all of them. King Fionn, Queen Niamh and Luna bade the group farewell from the drawbridge. The Queen embraced Calia with tears in her eyes before sobbing into Evander's shoulder. The King comforted her after giving his son, and heir, a tight embrace. Luna and Astrid clasped each other closely, whispering so only the other could hear, before Luna gave Calia a hug too.

The group travelled on horseback and two horses pulled the jail on wheels. Torin refused to travel inside it until they approached the entrance to Aldric. Anguish showed on Calia's hard-set face and the way she nervously squeezed her hands. Evander wanted nothing more than to take those hands and reassure her he would protect her and Torin, but he felt responsible for the situation and the torment she was feeling. Plus, Calia hadn't shown warmth towards him since Caradin's reply, and he knew she lay blame on him for Torin being in danger. If Evander had never desired the Silver Stag and followed him through the Woodland, none of this would have happened.

Dunkley rode beside Evander. 'You seem troubled.'

'Am I no better than Caradin? Coveting that which is most prized among hunters?' Evander wondered.

'Well, you haven't trapped an entire Kingdom inside a deathly fog, so no, I don't see any comparison here.' Dunkley offered.

'I had a desire to be victorious where others had failed. I wanted the glory.'

'A desire for glory does not make you evil, Ev. You could have taken your prize back at the cabin in the woods. But you chose to show mercy. That is what defines your character, my friend.'

Evander glanced in Calia's direction. 'Before I met her, I never even considered how I was perceived by others. But now, the only thing I want is to prove myself worthy.'

Dunkley chuckled. 'Most people just buy flowers or jewellery. But a mission to save an entire kingdom from a maniac works too.'

Calia rode alongside Torin for the duration of their journey. A large part of her longed for the solace of their home in the Woodland. Especially as they travelled the path which led them directly through the forest and out into the land of Aldric. The remoteness of their sanctuary and the life they had lived there, now felt like a different lifetime, something from long ago. Calia wished they could be back there now, in the safety of their solitude.

Sensing her unease, Torin tried his best to calm his sisters' nerves.

We are doing the right thing. We have a good plan, sister.

Calia shook her head. 'We have no plan for the protection of you. Caradin could have you locked in a dungeon as soon as we arrive.'

I will still be alive in a dungeon, and safe.

'And what if she orders you killed on sight? What then, brother?' Calia couldn't keep the anguish from her voice.

Evander will do what he can to prevent that from happening. You just need to stay focused so you can destroy the staff. No one will be able to get near Caradin until it's destroyed.

Calia fought back tears. His words did nothing to dispel the weight of dread which filled her insides.

~

The next morning, a sombre mood had settled over the party as today they would reach the entrance to Aldric. Calia couldn't watch as Torin entered the cage, nor as the curtains were lowered down over each side to spare him being stared at.

The path out of the Woodland which lead to the Kingdom of Aldric was deserted and run down. Overgrown tree branches hung low, while weeds and unkempt shrubs threatened to swallow what remained of the old, muddy road. When a damp fog became present in the air, Evander gave word that it was time to enact the first part of the plan.

'Dunkley, it is time to disappear and Calia, it is time to take his form.'

'Here goes nothing!' Dunkley popped the red sweet into his mouth and crunched loudly. Immediately his image began to fade into nothingness. Before he vanished completely, he took a seat on a small step which had been built into the back of Torin's cage.

'Are you ready?' Evander asked Calia. They had barely spoken two words since they'd set out. Calia held a small vial of yellow liquid in her hand, staring at it.

'It's not too late to change your mind,' Evander said, placing his hand over hers, covering the vial.

Calia looked into his eyes. 'I'm not changing my mind. I just can't help but feel something terrible is going to happen once we cross through the fog.'

'I can't promise you that everything will go perfectly to plan, but I can promise you that I will do everything in my power to keep Torin safe.' Evander gave Calia's hand a reassuring squeeze.

We're doing the right thing, sister. Caradin must be stopped. This is what mother and father would want us to do.

Calia went to raise the vial to her lips, as Evander stopped her. 'Just one more moment.'

She frowned as he cupped her cheek with his warm hand. 'Just one last moment to remember your face before you turn into my not-so-beautiful best friend.'

Calia couldn't help but smile and release a tense laugh, then she tipped the contents of the vial into her mouth and swallowed the bitter-tasting liquid.

Part 4

Dark Hearts and Starlight

The lingering fog grew denser with every minute, as the party walked in an alert silence, keeping their eyes and ears peeled for a sign of a soldier or guard. But they need not have worried. Not a soul was to be seen until they reached a clearing, where several armed guards stood to attention before a gaping hole in the mist. They held staffs lit at one end as torches against the swirling fog. Each one of them stood stock still, glaring at the approaching group. One large man stepped forward to greet them, his crooked nose and dark eyes could be seen from under his helmet, a bushy brown beard covered his mouth and neck.

'State your name and business for approaching Caradin's Kingdom of Aldric,' the man said, his voice as rough as his unpolished armour.

'I am Prince Evander, of Caedryn. I've been invited to meet with Queen Caradin,' Evander's voice was firm, but calm.

'In order to pass beyond the border, you must produce your invitation for proof,' the guard barked, eyeing each member of the party in turn.

Evander pulled a scroll from his saddle bag, dismounted and closed the distance towards the guard, handing him the parchment. The guard unrolled it and turned to another guard, nodding in his direction. He stepped forward and held out his torch, igniting the parchment. It immediately burned with a green flame before disintegrating into ash.

Upon seeing the shocked faces of Evander and his company, the guard eyed Evander, 'Fret not, you passed the queen's test. What's in the crate?' The guard nodded to the cage holding Torin.

'A gift for the Queen, at her request, the infamous Silver Stag.' Evander strode towards the cage and lifted the curtain on one side. All of the guards strained their necks to catch a glimpse of the famed creature. Murmurs of interest and fascination filtered out from the guards before their leader scolded them back to attention.

'So, the rumours are true?' the guard asked.

Evander nodded, 'I captured the beast two weeks ago and have offered the prize to Queen Caradin, as a sign of good faith in my intention to marry her daughter.'

The guard stared at Evander in surprise. 'You intend to marry Princess Avaleen? Are you mad?'

'That is my intent, correct.'

'Forgive my boldness, your highness. But do you realise you'll be enslaved to Caradin forever, she'll hold power over you until the day you die!' The guard's dark eyes were now wide in astonishment.

'My objective is to unite our kingdoms together, in the hope to bring peace.'

The guard scoffed and shook his head. 'Good luck to you and your intent, young prince. There's not many who go into Aldric and make their way out at all, let alone unscathed.'

'I heed your warning, but I wish to proceed. We've kept the queen waiting long enough.'

The guard performed a quick head count before waving the party through the opening in the fog, but not before issuing one final warning. 'Don't stray off the path until you're clear of the fog, or no one will ever be seeing you again!'

Four guards on horseback led the party towards the castle. The further away from the gap in the mist they travelled, the lighter it became. Calia took in her surroundings with wide eyes, not a lot looked familiar yet, but she was relieved to see that the sun was shining as the lingering mist evaporated. The castle loomed before them, and although Calia knew she had lived there for the first eight years of her life, she supposed she hadn't spent much time looking at the castle from this direction. The village before them was busy with people milling about, walking with baskets or pulling wagons, but Calia noticed they were not talking or smiling like in the marketplace. Everyone kept their eyes downcast, save for a quick glance at the approaching group and cart.

As they made their way through the town, Calia began to recognise a few buildings and was disheartened to see them run down. Thatched roofs showed gaps and patches, torn curtains hung in windows with crooked shutters. The clothes the villages wore seemed old and mended with visible stitching.

When they reached the gates of the castle, Calia finally felt a sense of familiarity. She could see the smaller gate set in the side of the wall where she and Torin had escaped so many years ago. She felt a clench in her stomach as she thought of Avaleen and what she would be like now. Would she be cold and bitter like her mother? Would she be tethered to a demon now and practicing dark magic to keep the Kingdom of Aldric locked down? Would there be any signs of the timid, but kind girl she had cared for like a sister?

At the castle entrance, six new guards greeted them, waving off the scruffy ones from the fog. These guards wore uniforms that were clean and new, neatly pressed under light armour which gleamed in the sunlight. A concierge stepped forward, immaculately presented, and bowed low.

'Prince Evander, I welcome you to the castle of Aldric. The Queen eagerly awaits you in the hall. This way.' He motioned for them to follow him as they dismounted. Evander led the way, followed by Astrid, and Calia disguised as Dunkley. The rest of the party heaved on the ropes to drag Torin and his cage inside.

Calia tried to rein in her wonderment at entering her old home. While the structure was the same, the interior had changed a lot. Gone were the red and gold velvet she remembered, replaced with emerald green and black instead. No longer did framed paintings of her family and ancestors hang on the walls, but instead elaborate portraits of Caradin hung in their place. Every painting depicted the Queen in a stance of power, staring stone faced and determined at anyone who laid eyes on her. The only thing which remained the same was the stone floor, their footsteps echoing around them.

The doors to the grand hall were opened before them, revealing an expansive space. Flaming sconces lined each wall, while an enormous, glittering chandelier hung low in the centre over an intricate woven carpet runner in green and black. Armoured soldiers stood to attention along the length of carpet. Before them, atop a staired platform, seated upon a carved mahogany throne, sat Caradin, grasping her sable-black staff. Her pale face was set in a firm expression, with her dark hair loose and a bejewelled golden crown upon her head. She wore an elaborate woven gown in ebony and gold, which clung to her slender frame, exposing ample cleavage and a small waist. Calia thought she hadn't changed at all in the past ten years and a cold shiver ran down her back.

When they reached the foot of the stone steps, Evander dropped to one knee and bowed low. The rest of the party followed suit. 'Queen Caradin, it is an honour to have been invited into your kingdom.'

Caradin rose from the throne and eyed the group, before settling her gaze on Evander. 'The Prince of Caedryn, I presume?'

'Yes, your highness. I am Prince Evander of Caedryn.'

If Evander was nervous, it didn't show. Calia on the other hand felt physically weak, her legs like jelly. Being in the presence of Caradin set off the anxiety from her childhood she thought she had long escaped. She squeezed her hands into fists and released them, over and over, while trying to keep her breath calm. She nearly jumped out of her skin when Dunkley's invisible hand grasped her wrist. They must be nearing the time of the spell wearing off. Calia glanced around, wondering how they would pull the switch off, with Caradin's soldiers lining the hall.

'You have courage, entering my Kingdom. Surely you have heard the rumours about the risk you and your group are taking?' Caradin asked with the slight curl of a smile.

Evander stood from his kneeling position. 'We understand that you are a wise and careful ruler, only trying to protect her Kingdom. You have given your word that no harm will come to us, and we believe you. My intent is to unite our kingdoms, for greater unity, and protection to both. The proposal of marriage to your daughter comes with the utmost sincerity on my behalf.'

'Hmm, sincerity you say? When a proposal was offered once before, you turned it down with no consideration at all. And now you expect me to believe you are worthy of marrying my only daughter?' Caradin's eyes turned dark as she glared at Evander.

'Your highness, I only ask for the opportunity to prove myself worthy of consideration. I admit I was foolish and immature to turn down your offer. But I have changed. I realise now the generosity and privilege which was offered, and only ask for a chance at redemption.'

Calia felt a trickle of sweat run down her neck as she squirmed in her heavy soldier's uniform, it felt hard to breathe. She was certain Caradin was about to order them all arrested.

'Trust is something which must be earned, do you understand that, young Prince?' Caradin frowned at Evander.

'I do, your highness, which is why I have kept my word in bringing you the gift you requested.' Evander motioned towards the covered cage.

Caradin turned to look behind her. 'Avaleen, come.'

There was movement behind the queen as two guards stepped aside to allow a young woman to step forward. Calia gasped as her beautiful stepsister, now grown like herself, stood beside her mother. Avaleen wore a long, fitted gown in a soft shade of jade green, her long auburn hair was worn loose over one shoulder, cascading down over the scarred side of her face, adorned with a delicate circlet of gold. Her downcast gaze and clasped hands gave Calia the impression Avaleen was still just as timid as before.

'My daughter may not have the strength and resolve I carry within me. But she does represent that which I value the most. Unwavering loyalty, obedience and reliability. I believe Avaleen will demonstrate these qualities as your wife, and in return I expect the same from you and your kingdom.'

Evander bowed in the direction of Avaleen. 'It is an honour to make your acquaintance, Princess Avaleen, and I very much look forward to getting to know you more.'

Avaleen offered a small curtsey to Evander, but made no eye contact.

Calia felt another tug on her arm, as Dunkley pulled her towards the back of the cage. She could begin to make out the faint outline of his body, and a new level of panic set in. The swap had to happen now, and they needed a distraction. Calia reached for the curtain hanging down the back of the cage, and flapped it, hoping it would be enough to alert Evander. She watched as Dunkley's faded image slipped underneath.

'Perhaps you would like to see your gift?' Evander said, the pitch of his voice elevated slightly. Evander turned to face the cage.

'Very well, let us see the legendary Silver Stag,' Caradin motioned for Evander to raise the coverings on the cage. Each of his soldiers did the same and Calia realised this was her opportunity and popped her red sweet into her mouth, and bit down hard. She disappeared under the back covering, and watched as Dunkley's form appeared completely in front of her eyes. He smiled and nodded at her as she looked down and realised her form had faded to invisible. Calia breathed a sigh of relief, before a collective gasp rang throughout the hall, and she thought they'd been sprung.

'What is the meaning of this?' Caradin's high-pitched screech rang throughout the hall.

Calia realised everyone was looking at the cage, and at first, she thought Caradin's outrage was caused by the empty cage, before she realised that it wasn't in fact empty. Lying in the bottom of the cage was the naked body of a young man with long, dark blonde hair, who appeared to be asleep.

Calia grasped the bars of the cage. It took all her restraint not to call out her brother's name. Silent tears of disbelief poured from her invisible eyes.

'Your highness, I assure you, when we entered your kingdom, the cage contained the silver stag. You can ask your guards; they saw it with their own eyes!' Evander cried; his cheeks flushed with colour.

Calia looked up at Caradin, expecting to see her face filled with the familiar darkness of anger she was so used to from her childhood. But what she saw was much worse. Caradin's mouth was twisted into the most wicked of smiles as she descended the steps. The soldiers stepped aside to allow her through, as Avaleen followed close behind.

'I had wondered, all these years, if the renowned silver stag was perhaps someone in disguise. And now my instincts have proven correct!' Caradin laughed, her voice tinged in malice. 'Here you are, home at last, dear stepson!'

Avaleen rushed to the edge of the cage, grasping the bars in mirror image to the invisible Calia. 'Torin?' she cried, her face bore a mixture of relief and hope, her single eye brimming with tears.

The human form in the cage stirred as though waking from a deep sleep, but couldn't quite rouse himself.

'I assure you; I had no idea of the stag's true form!' Evander cried, but Caradin seemed not to have heard him.

'I knew there was possibility it could be you. That is one of the reasons I crafted the barrier, to lift the enchantment should you return. But what of your dear sister?' Caradin appeared to be thinking out loud. 'With the true heir to the throne now laying here before us, this poses somewhat of a complication.' Finally, she turned her attention to Evander. 'I would be interested to know your thoughts on the matter.'

Evander understood this was a test. Caradin was challenging him to answer to determine his loyalty, and he chose his words carefully. 'If my understanding is correct, the former prince has been concealing himself as a stag for all these years?'

Caradin nodded for him to go on, the hint of her evil smile remained in place.

'Surely a man who has spent half of his life as a pitiful wild animal is not fit to rule. I would gladly endorse you to remain as sole ruler of the Kingdom of Aldric.'

Calia felt a body bump into her side and turned to find Dunkley beside her. 'Go!' he whispered under his breath. Calia looked at Torin's sleeping form in the bottom of the cage, and up to Evander who was focused on Caradin.

'With your daughter by my side, ruling alongside me as my equal, the Kingdoms of Aldric and Caedryn will be the most powerful, the strongest in all the land.' Evander said. 'And if the stag ever regains his voice back, I will interrogate him myself to determine what animal his sister has taken the form of, and ensure that species is eradicated from both our lands.'

His words stung, and Calia had to remind herself that he was lying to protect their cover. Calia took a careful step away from the cage, and another, ensuring not to make any sound.

Caradin clapped her hands together loudly. 'I believe preparations for a wedding should begin immediately!'

'But, Mother!' Avaleen cried, still clutching onto the cage.

'Stop snivelling, you ridiculous girl!' Caradin turned to her guards, 'Take the half man to the dungeon and have him locked away!'

'No!' Avaleen cried again.

'And take my daughter back to her chamber until she calms down. Evander and his party can be taken to the east wing and shown to their rooms. I have a wedding to plan!' Caradin whisked herself away while Avaleen was pulled by the arms to her room. Calia watched helplessly as several soldiers led Evander and his friends in the opposite direction, while another group broke down the door to the cage and dragged her brother away to be locked up yet again.

~

Calia felt torn. Part of her wanted to follow Torin down into the dungeons, and hide until he woke up so she could break him free. Now that he was human again, it would be easier to escape with him. To go back to their cabin in the Woodland. But that would mean deserting Evander, Astrid and Dunkley. The other part of her knew she had a job to do – to destroy Caradin's staff. In the end, duty to her kingdom, and new friends, won out. Calia set off up the stair case, to Caradin's chambers on the second floor. She dodged several castle staff members, none of whom looked familiar. Calia planned to sneak her invisible form into Caradin's room and take the staff.

Two guards stationed outside Caradin's heavy, wooden door posed the first challenge. Thinking quickly, Calia set off down another corridor, she seized a heavy porcelain vase on display and threw it to the ground. As the two guards came running towards the noise, she ran to Caradin's door. She gently pushed the door open to reveal the slightest possible crack for her to peer through.

Caradin had her back to the door. Calia slipped into the room, staying close to the wall. Even though she knew she was invisible, Calia felt safer remaining hidden behind the privacy screen. She kept her eyes glued to Caradin, standing amongst a ring of black candles, chanting incoherently as the flames grew larger around her. Calia held her breath. Unfolding before her was the scene her brother had described the night they escaped. Caradin was conjuring her demon.

As the chanting grew more fevered, the flames nearly hit the roof, and a black shadow emerged from the obsidian stone of the staff and joined Caradin within the circle, its form was grotesquely human in shape, but elongated and warped. Caradin dropped to her knees before it.

'Master, he has returned! The prince! We can finally complete our plan! I have him locked in the dungeons!'

'Well done. But you know it is not just him we need dead. Both the prince and princess must be dead for your claim to the throne to be complete and true.'

Caradin turned her face towards the wraith. 'You were right, the boy was the silver stag. But the girl's form still eludes us. We need to keep the prince alive until he can tell us what animal she became. Only then will we be able to hunt her down.'

'And what of the other prince, from the next kingdom? Has he agreed to marry your daughter?'

'Yes, the stupid fool. He's desperate to prove himself, and his loyalty.'

The demon's form flared larger. 'Very well. See the wedding goes ahead without fail. Once they are married, I can claim her as my vessel and we can leave this land, expanding our reign beyond these borders.' The wraith rasped.

Calia stood frozen, witnessing the horror and what it meant.

'You know, I would gladly host you within myself, dark lord, just say the word,' Caradin bowed before her master.

'Two hosts are better than one, and will allow our power to reach further. Your loyalty will not go unrewarded. I will bind part of myself to you to ensure you have constant access to my power even without the sceptre.'

'Thank you, master.'

Caradin stood and unlaced the front of her dress, allowing it to slip down her shoulders, revealing her breasts. The demon lowered its head to her chest and pressed its ephemeral form against her. Caradin cried out in a mixture of pain and ecstasy as she rose from the ground. The demon convulsed, transporting part of its form into her. Caradin gasped loudly, her hair billowing in a swirl of dark mist. As the demon pulled away, Caradin fell to her knees, panting.

'You would do well do keep your senses alert and your eyes open. I sense the girl is closer at hand than you think. I can smell her. And there's nothing beast-like about her scent at all,' the demon crackled, its form now smaller than before.

'What are you saying?' Caradin asked, redressing herself.

'I don't believe the girl ever succumbed to your spell. But I do believe she is here...somewhere. Perhaps in this very room!' The demon's voice faded to silence as it was sucked back into the staff, which Caradin hastily grasped again.

Calia dared not move as her heart pounded against her chest. She didn't risk even a single breath. Caradin glared around her room, suspicious malice emanating from her focused gaze. She began pacing, swinging her sceptre, in the hope of colliding with something which could not be seen.

As she made her way to the opposite side of the room, near the window, Calia seized her opportunity to slip through the door again, and then she ran.

~

Torin sat naked on the cold, stone floor of his cell. His back rested against the rough, rocky wall while his head drooped between his knees. He still felt groggy and could barely remember anything since they went through the gateway into Aldric, up until when he partially woke while being dragged by armoured guards, down into the dungeons. The cold barely even bothered him, and if it were not for the current situation, he would have relished being human again.

The light clicking of footsteps walking in his direction caused Torin to raise his head, squinting in the dull lantern light, as a figure stopped outside the bars to his cell. He expected to see a guard, but instead was met with the image of a stunning young woman, with alabaster skin and a cascade of auburn hair partially covering her face. A single green eye, rimmed with dark lashes, stared at him shyly, before holding out folded linens through the bars.

'Ava?' Torin's voice came out in a rasp. A pink blush filled her cheeks as Torin stood, reaching for the clothes, and she turned her head the other way.

'Oh, right. I'm human now,' Torin chuckled, as he pulled some loose pants on. He quite liked the fact he had made her blush. 'You can look now.'

Avaleen turned back, grasping the bars between them. 'Is it really you?'

'Just pretend were playing hide and seek. Now close your eye and count, as high as you know,' Torin repeated the last words he ever spoke to her. And she did close her eye, but only to stop the rush of tears which threatened to spill.

'Don't cry, Ava. You know I can't stand it,' Torin clasped her hands holding the bars. They felt incredibly soft and delicate, and he savoured the sensation after so long of feeling nothing with his former hooves.

Ava looked up at him. 'I thought you were dead. Mother always guessed you were the Silver Stag, but I didn't believe her. I was sure you had both died out in the wilderness. But what of Calia, is she alive?'

Torin grew wary for a moment and withdrew his hands. His heart told him he could trust Ava, but his head reminded him that she'd been living with Caradin for ten years and anything could have happened in that time.

Sensing his apprehension, Ava withdrew her own hands. 'You don't trust me. I understand. I wouldn't either.'

'Ava, I want to trust you. I want to believe we still have each other's backs after all this time, but I also know your mother is evil, and capable of anything if it means she can get what she wants. And right now, I'm her biggest threat.'

'No one fears my mother more than I. No one understands more about what she is capable of.' Ava stepped back, balling her hands into fists. 'I've lived in fear every day since you left. I've lived in this castle as a prisoner and I've watched her kill countless innocent people for trying to escape or stand up to her. I don't know if anyone can stop her at this point!' Ava's voice had become shrill and she took a deep breath.

'You may have had to live your life as a stag, but at least you were able to live freely. I'm going straight from one prison and into another.'

'What do you mean?' Torin asked, feeling alarmed. He still felt an innate protectiveness over her.

'Prince Evander. Mother is forcing me to marry him so she can take hold over his kingdom. I don't know why exactly, but I know she needs me to marry the prince so she can use me as some sort of pawn in her plan. I should have escaped with you and Calia when I had the chance, no matter if it cost me my life. It would be worth it, for a moment of freedom from her.'

'Have you told her you don't want to marry him?' Torin asked. But he knew the answer as soon as the words left his mouth.

'Would it matter?' Ava cried, and threw her arms in the air. The look of utter defeat and hopelessness on her face told him everything he needed to know. He reached for her through the bars.

'Ava,' Torin watched as she recoiled, wrapping her arms around herself. 'Ava, please.'

She stepped just close enough that he could grasp one of her hands.

'Ava, we have a plan. To free you, to free everyone.' He pulled her closer.

'What do you mean?' she asked, looking up at him through long dark lashes.

Torin reached up and cupped her cheek, brushing her hair away from her scarred eye. 'We have both been victims of your mother's cruelty, and I will not let her harm you, or anyone else again.'

'You know she plans to kill you?' Ava's voice caught in her throat. 'As long as you're alive she isn't truly the Queen, and I'm not truly a princess. She'll do it before the wedding ceremony, so there's no way Prince Evander can claim the wedding isn't legitimate later on.'

'Prince Evander isn't what you think. He knows exactly what is going on. And no offence, but he doesn't want to marry you either.'

Ava smiled slightly and pressed her cheek into Torin's palm. 'Am I that undesirable?'

'Not at all,' he answered, stroking her cheek. 'It's just that he's in love with Calia and is going through all this for her.'

Ava's eyes widened, and she stood up straight. 'Calia's alive then?'

'Very much so.'

Ava's face broke out into a radiant, relieved smile at the news.

Torin smiled with her. 'And we are all here to end Caradin's reign once and for all.'

~

Calia ran as fast as she could, hurling herself down the staircase, racing across the foyer towards the east wing. She took the next flight of stairs two at a time, stopping halfway to rest her aching thigh muscles, before taking off again. As she ran past a gilded mirror in the hall, she caught an image of her transparent reflection and glanced down at her returning form. She ran to the last door in the hall, the finest suite which was traditionally reserved for visiting royalty, and prayed it was the right room. As she burst through the door she collided directly into Evander, causing them both to fall to the floor. Calia lay sprawled across his chest, laying her head down for a moment to catch her breath.

'Thank goodness it's you,' they both said in unison, meeting each other's gaze and smiling awkwardly. Calia scrambled to her feet and offered a hand to Evander.

'We have a problem,' Calia started, brushing her tangled hair away from her face. Evander strode past to lock the door before turning back to her.

'I guess that means you weren't able to destroy the staff?'

Calia shook her head. 'Caradin never let it go. But that's not all. I saw her summon the demon, and she let it infuse some of its *matter* into her. Destroying the sceptre won't be enough.'

Evander frowned. 'We have to destroy her as well.'

'There's more,' Calia said, sitting on the edge of Evander's bed. 'Caradin knows I'm here. Her demon sensed me.'

'But has she seen you?'

'No, not yet.'

Evander came to sit beside her on the bed. 'That's something at least. You can still hide from her.'

'But it may be a potential problem for you, if she believes you know. Before the demon sensed me, Caradin told him she had you eating out of her hand, that you're desperate to prove your loyalty to her. But now she has reason to believe you've been deceiving her.'

Evander grasped Calia's hand, pulling her close. 'I don't want you to worry about me. I'll alert Astrid and Dunkley and let them know that the priority is to kill Caradin, not just destroy her staff.'

Calia looked up into Evander's eyes. 'I don't want anything to happen to you. You are already risking so much being here in the first place.' She held his gaze for a moment. 'Caradin is going to let the demon possess Ava after you are married, so that it can travel to your kingdom and take over.'

Evander nodded thoughtfully. 'Which must mean it can't leave without a human body to host it. This is good, Calia. The more we know, the better chance we have of defeating them. Do you think Avaleen is aware of her mother's plan?'

Calia shrugged. 'Ava looked so relieved to see Torin alive. I hope she hasn't been turned by her mother's evil ways. But we've been gone so long, it's hard to know.'

'We know one thing for sure, Caradin needs me alive for her plan to work. So, you don't need to worry about me.' Evander smiled down at Calia, gently stroking her cheek.

'Please just promise me you'll do whatever it takes to keep yourself safe. Especially if something happens to me. Go through with the wedding if you have to. If it means it will get you home alive, please just do it.' Calia's eyes filled with tears at the prospect of Evander leaving for Caedryn with Avaleen as his wife.

Evander chuckled. 'I have no intention of going through with the wedding, Calia. I plan for Caradin to be gone before it comes to that.'

'But...' Calia started. Evander held up a finger gently to her lips.

'I only plan to be married once in my life, and the woman I plan to marry captured my heart the moment I laid eyes on her, selling wildflowers in a market place.'

Calia pressed her cheek into his palm, blushing.

'When all this is over, is there a possibility you would consider marrying me?' Evander asked, his eyes full of hope.

Calia's heart fluttered. 'Of course, there is. But there's so much at stake, I can't think about that now.'

Evander bent his head closer towards Calia's. 'Then for this moment, just think about this,' he gently pressed his lips against her own. She returned the kiss, softly at first, tentative. As her heart began to race, she wrapped her hands around the back of his neck and pulled him closer, opening her mouth, inviting more. Evander kissed her harder and ran his hands up both of Calia's arms, grasping her shoulders and running his hands down the length of her back, stopping at her waist, before pulling her closer. Calia pressed herself against his chest, arching her back and tangling her fingers into his dark hair. Evander reached under her jacket and shirt until his hands found the soft skin underneath, delicate and warm. He lightly traced his fingers along her back and across her stomach and relished the shiver she released. Calia grasped the collar of Evander's shirt, pulling him over her as she lay back. A commotion in the hall outside caused them both to freeze. Fists banging loudly on doors, and voices shouting.

'What's going on?' Calia jumped up from the bed, straightening her clothes.

'I don't know, but you better hide just in case. Wait,' Evander tugged on her hand before she could move away, and quickly kissed her lips. 'Go, out on the balcony.'

Calia slipped through the curtains, and through the door out into the cold night air. Her flushed skin shivered in the brisk breeze. She heard Evander unlock his door and open it to the turmoil down the hall. Caradin's voice carried out loud and shrill.

'Search everywhere! Remember she's invisible. Slash and poke with your blades. Under beds, behind doors and curtains. Leave no space unchecked!'

'What is going on?' Evander demanded.

'It seems we have an intruder in the castle. An invisible one,' Caradin crowed. 'Let in by you!'

'What are you talking about?' Evander asked.

Calia held her breath, leaning against the railing of the balcony. She knew she wasn't safe, even out here, and glanced around for somewhere else to go.

'Calia, Torin's sister, is running around the castle, invisible. No doubt trying to destroy me!' Caradin's voice was manic. 'Why did you bring her here?'

'I honestly have no idea what you're talking about, your highness. My intention was to prove myself worthy of your daughter, that is all. I brought the stag as a gift, at your request.' Evander certainly sounded convincing but Calia couldn't tell if Caradin believed him or not. 'Please, search my room, I have nothing to hide.' Evander said loudly.

Calia watched as a guard stabbed his sword out from the doorway, curtains billowing. She quickly climbed over the edge of the railing, grateful for the foot-wide ledge bordering the castle wall. Pressing herself flat against the wall, like Torin had shown her many years ago, Calia edged along the border until she reached the corner of the wall, carefully stepping around to the other side. There were no other balconies on this side, and the next window was several meters away, if it was even open. She would have to wait until the coast was clear to creep back to Evander's room.

Evander stepped aside, allowing Caradin to pass by him, she eyed him warily. 'And what if the girl is found? You realise her claim to the throne comes before mine, or Avaleen's?'

'How can anyone prove she is who she claims to be? It's been far too long for anyone to recognise her. My intention remains the same. What you choose to do with an invisible intruder and a stag who turned into a dishevelled man is up to you. It is *your* kingdom after all.'

Even though Calia knew he was lying, Evander's words caused a sinking feeling deep inside her stomach. It would be so easy for him to betray her.

'I've decided the wedding will take place tonight, under the full moon. And if that girl doesn't show herself before the moon reaches its peak, Torin's throat will be slit before the ceremony begins.'

Caradin and Evander eyed each other while her guards searched his room.

'This entire wing is clear. There's no sign of the girl.' Reported a guard standing to attention.

'Keep soldiers posted outside every room, with doors locked, until it is time for the ceremony to begin!' Caradin barked. 'Now, take me to my daughter. It's time for her to get ready for her wedding.'

Once Caradin was gone, and the door locked behind her, Evander rushed out to the balcony. 'Calia?' He whispered, peering over the edge, looking for a sign of her.

Calia edged her way back around the wall corner.

'Oh my god! Calia!' Evander exclaimed, reaching for her as a piece of the ledge gave way. She lost her footing for a moment but was able to regain her balance. Calia reached for Evander's outstretched hand. He grasped her fingers, and pulled her towards him, helping her over the railing, before pulling her into a tight embrace. Movement on the next balcony saw Astrid waving her arms at them. She shrugged and frowned, to ask what was going on. The expanse was too far for them to speak without being overheard. They could see Dunkley out on his balcony in the distance.

'I'll go across and fill her in, and then go over to Dunkley and tell him,' Calia said.

Evander shook his head. 'It's too dangerous. I'll write it down and throw the message across.' He disappeared inside, before returning with a blanket. 'Here, you'll have to wait outside in case someone checks the room.' He wrapped the blanket around Calia's shoulders. 'The sun's almost down and it's getting cold.'

Calia took the blanket gratefully and watched as he rustled around the room, searching for what he needed. He returned to the balcony to write the note, before wrapping it around a heavy, ceramic bowl from the dresser, and fastening it with ribbon from the drawer. Evander threw the package confidently, and Astrid easily caught it. She nodded to show her understanding, before tossing the package to Dunkley.

'Now what do we do?' Calia asked, gazing up at the darkening sky.

'Now, we wait.' Evander pulled Calia down beside him, wrapping his arms around her. Calia lay her head on his shoulder as the first stars twinkled to make their presence known. She felt more calm staring at the open sky and hoped that Torin was safe in his cell, and that he had a window in which he could gaze at the starlight too.

~

Avaleen sat in her window seat, watching the night sky. Her thoughts were dominated by her visit with Torin in the dungeon. She had dreamt about finding him one day, alive and well. But never in her wildest dreams had she thought he would come back to the castle, to rescue her from the cruelty of her mother. He was even more handsome than she imagined, with his dark-blonde hair in waves past his shoulders and deep blue eyes. Her cheeks burned as the image of his naked body came into her mind. She had wanted so badly to reach out and run her hand along his muscled chest and stomach. A feeling of desire washed over her like she had never felt before, a longing deep inside that made her ache and close her eyes, picturing Torin reaching for her, holding her against his body, while he run his other hand down along her skin, reaching toward the place her desire yearned for him to touch.

The turning of a key in the lock to her door startled Avaleen out of her daydream. Her mother entered, flanked by two guards.

'It turns out we have an invisible spy making herself at home inside *our* castle,' Caradin announced loudly, glancing around Avaleen's room. The guards fanned out, striking and jabbing the air with their swords.

Calia. Avaleen thought.

'I've been locked inside, alone. I don't see how anyone could be hiding in here,' Avaleen said, turning to her mirror and fixing her hair over her scar. Her mother hated it showing just as much as Avaleen herself did.

'The wedding is being moved to tonight, as the moon reaches its fullest and highest point in the sky. I'm sick of all these surprises.' Caradin said, coming to stand behind her daughter.

Avaleen gaped at her mother's reflection in the mirror. 'Mother, no! I've told you I don't want to marry the prince. I don't even know him! He could be horrible; he could be a murderer!' Avaleen cried.

Caradin smiled a twisted smile. 'It hardly matters my dear, does it? The goal is to take over the kingdom of Caedryn, not ride off into the sunset!'

'Please don't make me do this, mother.'

Caradin squeezed her daughter's shoulders. 'Once you are married, a world of opportunity and power opens up for us. I'll show you how to harness that power, show you how you can have anything you want.'

Avaleen shook her head. 'I don't want any of what you're talking about. Marrying the prince means I can't have the only thing I actually do want.'

Caradin's face turned dark. 'Torin dies tonight, *darling*. What you want won't even be an option. You've been besotted with that boy since we moved here! It's pathetic! His presence only stops us from gaining all the power we ever desired!'

'No mother. It stops you from getting what you want. I've never wanted any power. I am nothing like you.'

Caradin narrowed her eyes, staring at Avaleen through the mirror. 'You're right. We are nothing alike. You are weak and useless. And still I've put up with your existence. Fed you, clothed you, kept you safe.' Her fingers dug deeper into Avaleen's shoulders. 'A little bit of gratitude wouldn't go astray, you selfish little bitch!' Caradin hissed her words, before grabbing Avaleen's hair and pulling it back so hard Avaleen had no choice but to meet her mother's stare, her neck felt like it might snap.

'You will watch as Torin has his throat sliced open, and bleeds out on the ball room floor. And then you will marry the prince. Afterwards, you will consummate your marriage during a ceremony I will conduct in my own chambers. Then you will be exposed to the greatest power you have ever known.'

Caradin released her hold on Avaleen's hair, and stormed from the room, locking the door behind her. Tears spilled down Avaleen's cheek as she raced to the balcony. She glared down at the garden below her, rubbing her aching neck. She could still feel the imprint of her mothers' fingers in her shoulders.

One jump. She thought. *One jump and this entire ordeal will be over. I will be free.* Avaleen grasped the railing and lifted her leg over the top. But the railing was cold, like the bars to Torin's cell, and the image of him filled her mind, along with the touch of his hand on hers. Avaleen lowered her leg and closed her eyes against the cold night air.

They have a plan. To be free from her once and for all.

Avaleen prayed that Torin was right, that his plan would work, before her mother could kill him. And if it didn't, at least she had her own plan, should all else fail. She squeezed the railing of the balcony before turning away to prepare for her unwanted wedding.

~

The moon was high in the sky when the guards came for Evander. He had heard them coming and made sure to be in the room, leaving Calia to hide on the balcony. He had a dagger hidden inside his boot, to attack Caradin at the first opportunity. As Evander hoped, the guards led him out without a second look at his room, and marched him down the hall. Dunkley and Astrid were being led ahead of him, flanked by guards of their own.

In the ballroom, a small crowd was assembled along each wall. Most were guards, but there were also several people who looked as though they worked in the castle, and some from the village. Torin stood chained and guarded at the base of the steps, leading up to the platform where Caradin sat in her throne. She looked every bit the dark queen in a sleek, low-cut, black lace and satin gown, twirling her sceptre. Her chestnut-coloured hair was piled high and elaborate upon her head, adorned with a sparkling crown encrusted with diamonds and emeralds. Two guards stood behind her, and an ancient looking priest beside her, wearing robes of white and maroon. He held a large, leather-bound tome in his frail looking hands. Astrid and Dunkley were stationed amongst the rest of their party, surrounded by soldiers.

Evander wasn't sure what to do next. He tried not to acknowledge Torin, and instead gazed at Caradin. She eyed him with a bitter smile.

'You may approach,' she cooed.

Evander began to climb the stairs, the rigid shaft of his dagger pressing against his ankle. Caradin straightened in her chair.

'I'd say it's about time we begin.' She waved her hand, and music began playing by a small band stationed by the doorway. The priest looked up, startled, and quickly turned to the page in his book, ignoring Evander. The doors to the ballroom opened to reveal Avaleen, waiting. She looked beautiful, Evander thought, in a long, fitted, white gown which pooled around her feet. Her strawberry-coloured hair fell in waves around her face. But Evander could tell she wasn't smiling. In fact, she looked terrified. It made Evander nauseous. He knew he was doing this for Calia, and for Torin, and the kingdom of Aldric. But this poor girl seemed to be nothing more than a pawn in her mother's evil game. Evander took a deep breath and willed his nerves to turn into courage for what he must do. He only hoped the right opportunity would present itself before it was too late.

Avaleen made her way down the aisle, avoiding eye contact with the prince and her mother. Instead, she looked at Torin, chained but determined. His eyes returned her gaze and he nodded ever so slightly. Taking a deep breath, she ascended the stairs to meet her future husband.

~

Calia waited until the guards had left with Evander before checking the room. She crept silently towards the door, glancing out to make sure no one was still in the hall. Unfortunately, two guards were stationed at the other end, blocking the staircase. She frowned, trying to think of another way down.

Of course! She smiled and turned to her right, remembering the dumb-waiter in the wall. Torin and her would often hide in there when they were children, waiting to scare unsuspecting maids. Sliding open a panel in the wall to reveal the cavity, she hoped she would still fit. Calia tugged on the pulleys until the platform reached her, turning to look up at the space above. She would have to stand to fit inside now, and hoped she could hold her own weight. Once inside, Calia used the pulleys to lower herself down the two floors until she reached the kitchen. It sounded quiet, so using her foot to slide open the door, she pushed her feet out first and landed with a loud and painful bump on the bench in the castle's kitchen, only to be met by a hunched and rounded woman brandishing a large knife.

'Who in the devil are you?' The woman demanded.

'Chevlon?' Calia asked, holding up her hands. 'It's me, Calia.'

The woman's face softened. 'The invisible intruder I suppose?' she asked, her eyes full of shiny tears.

'That would be me, yes.'

Chevlon pulled Calia off the bench and into a tight bear hug, tossing her knife aside.

'Oh, thank the stars. Thank the stars. Just look at you! All grown up, and so beautiful, even if you are dressed like a man!'

Calia laughed and hugged the older lady back. 'And you haven't changed one bit!'

'But what are you doing here? It's not safe. The wedding has started, and that evil witch has your brother in chains, and is about to have him killed! And you'll be next if she catches you in here!'

Calia explained as fast as she could what was happening, and that she needed to get as close to Caradin as she could, in the hope of killing her before she harmed Torin.

'You'll do no such sneaking up dressed like that,' Chevlon indicated to Calia's soldier's uniform. 'Best you blend in like the rest of us.' Chevlon went to a cupboard and fetched a folded uniform worn by the maids of the castle. Hastily, the two stripped Calia of her old uniform, and into the new one.

'Here, you'll be needing this,' Chevlon handed Calia the large knife she'd been brandishing moments before, and showed Calia where to hide it in her apron. Handing Calia a tray of candles, she said, 'There's a table, behind the main platform. You can pretend to be lighting and changing them over.' Quickly tucking Calia's hair inside a bonnet and pulling it down low on her face, Chevlon ushered Calia out of the kitchen, towards the back entrance of the dining hall.

Calia could hear music playing, as she crept through the passageway and into the ballroom. She entered behind the platform and could see Caradin upon her throne, flanked by guards. An elderly priest beside her, and Evander in front. Avaleen was making her way down the aisle, looking miserable. Evander looked nervous. Calia continued to slip along the wall, towards the hall table, where several candelabra stood, and pretended to swap burned down candles for new ones. All the while, trying to work out how she could get to Caradin. She spotted Torin, chained and guarded, and felt her palms grow sweaty, fumbling with the candles. She needed a distraction. Looking up, Calia noticed a woven tapestry hanging above the table. She pushed the candelabra back as far as she could against the wall, and replaced the candle at the top with the longest one on her tray. The flame licked the bottom of the tapestry as Calia crept behind the gathered crowd and hid behind a stone pillar. She spied Astrid and Dunkley. As the tapestry caught fire, and people began to gasp, Calia ducked out, grasping Astrid's arm, pulling her close to the pillar.

'I need a distraction, to get to Caradin,' Calia hissed.

'Is this fire not the distraction?' Astrid whispered. The wedding guests were beginning to point and panic.

'It won't last long enough. You and Dunkley need to do something, please!' Calia urged. As the words left her mouth,

Caradin stood and pointed her staff at the half-burned wall hanging. A white mist emerged, dousing the flames.

'No need to panic, just stupidity at play. Someone will pay dearly for that!' Caradin yelled. Everyone immediately hushed and stood back in their positions.

'Shall I begin?' The priest asked, holding up his book. Avaleen had reached the podium and now stood beside Evander.

'Not just yet, we seem to be missing a guest.' Caradin glanced out amongst the crowd as Calia pressed herself against the pillar.

'I know you're out there Calia, show yourself!' Caradin's voice echoed throughout the ballroom, but was met with silence. Calia dared not move.

'Very well then. You leave me no choice. Guards!' Caradin waved towards the men holding Torin. 'Bring the boy here, so everyone can see him.' Caradin pointed to the base of the steps in front of her platform.

Torin's chains made a loud, grating raucous as he struggled against them. Two guards dragged him to where Caradin indicated.

'Let it be known, that I am the rightful ruler to the Kingdom of Aldric. I have earned my place upon this throne. And anyone who tries to take it from me, will meet their death. Kill him!'

As one guard raised his sword high, two others held Torin in place. Caradin stood with a wicked snarl upon her face, waiting for the moment the blade was brought down onto Torin's neck. Just before the sword dropped, Astrid shoved

Dunkley hard, sending him sprawling into the space before Torin.

'How dare you!' Astrid screamed, as Dunkley scrambled to his feet. Astrid shoved him again. The guard lowered his blade.

'What is the meaning of this?' Caradin raged. Calia took her opportunity to race back behind the crowd, to the back of the platform.

'I just found out this bastard has been cheating on me!' Astrid screamed, yanking a surprised Dunkley by the collar. She drew a hand back and slapped him hard across the face.

'Enough!' Caradin roared. 'Seize them!' Caradin's guards left her side and Calia took her opportunity. She charged up the stairs, kitchen knife in hand. Her heart pounded in her ears as she neared the top, Caradin's tall form in sight. Calia had killed plenty of small animals before. And she told herself this was no different. Caradin was evil and needed to be stopped. Calia reached the top, steps away. She raised her arm high, ready to bring it down into Caradin's back. As she made her final leap, Caradin turned and aimed her sceptre at Calia. A green flash escaped the obsidian stone, striking Calia in the chest, rendering her frozen in mid-air. Her knife cluttered to the floor.

A loud, malicious laugh reverberated throughout the hall. 'Ha!' Caradin screamed. 'How stupid do you think I am? I knew you'd show yourself eventually, you pathetic girl!' Caradin swung her sceptre around, and Calia with it, until both were pointing towards the stunned crowd. 'Now I have you both, right where I want you!'

Torin struggled, eyes locked on his sisters, as she hung precariously in the air above him.

Evander saw his opportunity and reached for the dagger in his boot. He approached Caradin from behind and in one swift move, grabbed her around the neck and shoulder, pressing the dagger firmly to her throat. 'Release them both now, or it is you who will die.'

Caradin cackled once again. 'You fool, I knew I couldn't trust you. And now you will know my true power!'

Caradin shook her sceptre, releasing Calia, who fell to the ground, down several steps. A black haze started to seep from the obsidian stone. Evander released his hold on Caradin and kicked as hard as he could at Caradin's arm, causing her to drop the staff. He kicked it down the steps where it landed with a shattering sound as the stone hit the hard tiled floor, smashing to pieces. The black haze began to disappear.

'No!' Caradin cried.

Evander went to grab Caradin again, but she turned around to face him, her eyes wide and wild. She held her hands out in front of her and made a shoving motion in the air, towards Evander, who was thrown backwards, hard against the heavy wooden throne. His head made a sickening thud against the leg, rendering him unconscious.

'None of you are any match for me!' Caradin yelled, throwing her head back and releasing a guttural cry. When she righted herself, her eyes had turned completely black. And the voice which emerged next did not sound like her own. 'Power from the most vehement dark lord runs through these veins. And we will stop at nothing to achieve what we desire most!' The voice was deep and gravelly. The gathered crowd cowered in fear, clutching at one another, even the guards seemed unsure at what to do now.

Caradin stepped to the edge of the platform and pointed down at Torin and Calia, both still held by guards. 'Let their blood spill upon this floor!'

Before the guards could raise their swords against the imprisoned brother and sister, Caradin gasped and clutched at her chest. She coughed once and blood began to spill from her lips. She stumbled and turned her back to the crowd, revealing the long wooden handle of a kitchen knife protruding from between her shoulder blades. And a determined looking Avaleen, gasping for breath.

'You're reign is over, mother. You are nothing.'

Caradin reached for her daughter, with a look of shocked disbelief. Avaleen stepped away, chest heaving, as tears began to trickle down her cheek. Caradin collapsed, sliding feet first down the stairs, before her body came to a stop in front of Torin and Calia.

'Is it over?' Calia asked, her voice felt small in the stunned silence of the ballroom. She glanced at Torin who shrugged at the guards holding his arms. They let go, looks of confusion on their faces. Suddenly all the guards released the people they were holding, and began clutching and shaking their heads.

'My mother has had you all under her command, using dark magic to control your minds. But she is now dead. You no longer answer to her!' Avaleen called out, then she turned to help up a dazed Evander. 'If it's alright with you, I'd like to call off this wedding?'

Evander smiled, then winced in pain as he stood to his feet. 'That is completely fine with me, I'm very sorry for pretending I wanted to marry you. I meant no disrespect.'

'I understand, and you are forgiven.'

Astrid and Dunkley raced up the stairs to assist Evander in making his way down off the platform.

Calia turned to her brother. 'Are you alright?'

'I will be, once I have these chains removed.' Torin turned to one of the guards who had been holding him. 'Would you mind?'

The guard unlocked the chains and Torin and Calia embraced.

'Is it true?' the guard asked. 'Are you Prince Torin? Returned to save us all?'

'I am, although I don't know about the saving part. I'm afraid I've spent the entire time locked up. But this is my sister, Calia. It is her, and Prince Evander you have to thank.'

'No,' said Calia. 'It is Ava who has saved us all.'

Everyone turned to look up at Avaleen, whose hands had begun to shake. The shock of what she had done sank in. 'I killed my mother. I am a murderer.' Avaleen sank to the ground.

'No, Ava. You are a hero.' Calia limped up the stairs to embrace her. Torin, a few steps behind, embraced them both, as Avaleen broke into loud, heavy sobs.

'What about the fog?' Evander asked.

Everyone in the room began talking excitedly, and rushing towards the castle doors. The people spilled out, pointing towards the forest in the distance. The heavy mist could be seen rising from the tops of the trees, now just a thin veil of cloud dissipating in the clear night sky, revealing thousands of stars and bright moonlight.

'The fog is gone!' Someone shouted from the crowd. 'We are free!'

A thunderous cheer went up from the crowd, as more of the castle staff emerged to witness the freedom for themselves. Chevlon embraced Torin and Calia, squeezing them tight. The band began playing a much more upbeat and merrier tune and people began dancing and cheering upon the castle steps.

'This really does call for a celebration,' Evander said over the noise, turning to Torin and Calia, who had linked arms with Avaleen. 'But it is your call, this is your castle now, your kingdom to command.'

Torin looked to Calia, who smiled and bowed in mock gesture, 'Your Highness.'

Torin laughed, then yelled 'I say, we celebrate!' The crowd cheered even louder.

~

The revelries continued long into the hours of the morning, when just after sunrise, troops from the Kingdom of Caedryn arrived, led by King Fionn. Queen Niamh and Princess Luna who had been staying in the next village, arrived a short time after, when word had been sent that the threat was gone. King Fionn crowned Torin as King of Aldric, and reinstated Princess Calia, as rulers over the newly freed Kingdom. Avaleen was cleared of any wrongdoing, but was stripped of her title as Princess, and instead declared a Lady of the Court and an Honorary Knight due to bravery and services to the Kingdom.

In the coming days, many of the people of Aldric fled the kingdom, seeking out their loved ones. Some people from neighbouring kingdoms, ventured into Aldric to find their lost family and friends, once word had spread that the wicked Queen Caradin was dead and the land was once again safe.

In the coming months, life began to return to the way it had been, before King Brennus had died. Torin had much to learn about being king and ruling over a kingdom. With constant guidance from King Fionn, and support from Evander who stayed on for several weeks, Torin found his way. Although, he often longed for the solitude and freedom of the Woodland, and whenever he found a few days in which to escape his duties, Torin would take Avaleen to his secret cabin in the forest where, for a moment, they could be a regular couple, without the trauma of their childhoods.

Within a year, Torin and Avaleen were married, with Avaleen expecting their first child, a spring baby, whom they both vowed to love and protect above all else. Together they ruled over Aldric, with kindness and fairness and became trusted and adored by their people.

Evander and Calia were married in an elaborate sunset ceremony shortly after returning to Caedryn. After honeymooning in the family's seaside palace, they returned to Caedryn to take over ruling from King Fionn and Queen

Niamh. King Evander gifted his sister Princess Luna a large plot of land for her eighteenth birthday, on the border of the Woodland, and had a large cottage built on it. Together with Astrid, they adopted several children and raised copious amounts of animals and lived very happily together.

While beginning a family of their own didn't happen as easily as it did for others, eventually Evander and Calia were blessed with twins, a boy and a girl, a brother and a sister. The Kingdoms of Aldric and Caedryn flourished for many years, side by side, once harmony was restored and the darkness of the past left behind them. The two families visited often, and always instilled the importance of caring and protecting each other so their children understood that the love of family can always overcome the greatest of evils.

And they all lived happily
ever after....
THE END

Acknowledgements

I'm very lucky to be blessed with a supportive family, who allow me the time and space to indulge my writing passion. Thank you to my husband and kids, who are always proud of me and encourage me to pursue my dreams.

Thank you to my amazing writing community, both in the real world and online. I feel so lucky to have connected with so many talented and supportive people, many who have become mentors and close friends. A special shout-out to Kristen for making the gorgeous cover and media graphics, your super-talented and I'm so grateful we connected!

Thank you to my wonderful Beta readers, for taking the time to read early versions of this story and provide feedback; Toni, Jonty, Kim, Jacky, Tamara. I truly appreciate your help.

And finally, I would like to thank the most spectacular readers and fans of my work. You will never know how completely you lift me up and fill me with such joy to know you have bought, downloaded and read my stories. And for everyone who takes the time to leave a review or send me a message to tell me you liked the story, my absolute thanks and gratitude goes to you.

Love and Light
Danielle xx

ABOUT THE AUTHOR

Danielle lives in Melbourne with her four gorgeous kids and wonderful husband. A lover of fantasy from a young age, Danielle has always enjoyed making up stories and daydreaming about magical lands. Her favourite books and movies growing up included Peter Pan, Alice in Wonderland, The Neverending Story, Harry Potter and the Shadowhunter world by Cassandra Clare.

Danielle loves writing enchanting and exciting tales full of magic and adventure for pre-teen and young-adult readers.

To keep in touch and access Danielle's other books, including The Mystica Trilogy, scan the QR below or go to:

https://linktr.ee/fourmoonspublishing

Other Works by Danielle Hughes